Janet Tuckey

Joan of Arc

The Maid

Janet Tuckey

Joan of Arc
The Maid

ISBN/EAN: 9783742818201

Manufactured in Europe, USA, Canada, Australia, Japa

Cover: Foto ©Andreas Hilbeck / pixelio.de

Manufactured and distributed by brebook publishing software
(www.brebook.com)

Janet Tuckey

Joan of Arc

JOAN OF ARC

"THE MAID"

BY JANET TUCKEY

"I shall be well content with any choice
Tends to God's glory and my country's weal."
King Henry VI.

THE·NEW·PLVTARCH

London:
MARCUS WARD & CO., 67, 68, CHANDOS STREET
AND ROYAL ULSTER WORKS, BELFAST
1880

e

PREFACE.

O F all stories in history, not one needs explanation or apology less than the story of Joan of Arc. The more simply it is told, the more must teller and listener alike be stirred to admiration and touched with pity.

Among heroines of history, this young girl stands foremost in a rare union of qualities. The soldier's courage, the patriot's devotion, the purity of a saint, and the constancy of a martyr, were all, in her, blended with and glorified by the very truest womanliness.

It seems, to one who has pondered long over the history of her life, as if she should hardly be offered for an example to us, so far did she go beyond our power of following. But even this brief record of her true and beautiful life may help to shame those who have known no aim higher than self-delight—whose lives are untrue and unlovely for lack of that honest goodness which made her what she was.

Those who desire to know her more fully, I would send to the French writers whose able and love-guided pens have shown her plainly to a world which had long misunderstood her. Among their numerous works, I would specially name the *Procès de Jeanne d'Arc*, in five volumes, edited by M. Jules Quicherat, and the temperate and sympathetic life of the Maid, by M. Henri Wallon.

J. T.

KEW, *January*, 1880.

CONTENTS.

Google

JOAN OF ARC.

CHAPTER I.

INTRODUCTORY.

IT was to a distracted and miserable land, to a country divided against itself, that our King Henry of Monmouth carried, in 1415, the unjust renewal of an ill-founded claim, and an army to support it.

Charles V. of France, whose wisdom had done more than arms to win back the provinces conquered by Edward the King and Edward the Prince during the first part of the Hundred Years' War, had died in 1380, leaving two boys, Charles the Dauphin and Louis of Orleans. The long minority of the young King, and the madness which afterwards overtook him, gave the Government into the hands of his uncles, who cared much for their own interests, and little for those of their country. The wisest of them, Philip, Duke of Burgundy, died in 1404, and his son, John the Fearless, became the personal enemy and political opponent of Louis of Orleans, who for some time had been trying to get a share in the Government. The rivalry between them ended in the murder of Louis by his cousin's orders. The murderer managed to extort pardon, and even a sort of approval, from the mad King, his victim's brother. Paris took his part, and the University set one of its ablest doctors to preach in defence of his crime. On the other hand, all who hated him, and were jealous of his power, combined against him. The Count of Armagnac made himself the avenger of Louis. Having married his daughter to the young Charles of Orleans, he marched towards Paris with his lawless southern bands, whom the north-French dreaded more than any foreign enemy. They overran the land, pillaging wherever they went, sparing neither priests nor women, churches nor abbeys. When in a jocular mood, they would cut off the ears and nose of any peasant they chanced to meet, and bid him " go show himself to his mad King."

Paris became a prey alternately to the Burgundians and Armagnacs, who vied with each other in taxing and oppressing the citizens. For in this the two parties were alike; they both regarded the people as creatures made only to be spoiled and ill-treated, and forced by any means, no matter how cruel, to minister to the pleasure or greed of their masters for the time being.

The struggle and the anarchy had lasted several years, when Henry of England took advantage of them to revive the claim of Edward III. on the French crown. A slighter pretext would have served the English: they longed for war; they were eager to renew the glories of Crecy and Poitiers—more eager, perhaps, to enrich themselves with the plunder of France.

Harfleur was soon taken, and Agincourt was won. Then Henry went back to England for fresh troops, and during his absence the rival parties, instead of uniting against him for their country's sake, grew more bitter in their selfish strife. The King's two elder sons having died within one year, Armagnac was accused of having poisoned them to make room for their brother Charles, a boy of fifteen, whom he could guide as he chose. The Queen, Isabeau of Bavaria, whose licentious life and cruel neglect of her poor husband had long scandalised the Parisians, was banished to Tours by the Dauphin's orders (1417). She never forgave this insult, but made friends with the Duke of Burgundy, and lost no opportunity of injuring her son and his party. Next year the Burgundians got possession of Paris, and there was a general massacre of the Armagnacs, in which the Count perished.

In the meanwhile Henry had returned, and was conquering Normandy. The Duke of Burgundy

attempted to negotiate with him, but Henry's condi-
tions were too hard, and the Duke, angry at his
failure, was induced to become reconciled to the
Dauphin. A true alliance between them would have
saved France ; but at their second interview, held on
the bridge of Montereau, John was assassinated by
the Dauphin's attendants. It is uncertain whether
Charles had actually instigated the crime, but it is
certain that he inflicted no punishment on the
criminals.

The people of Paris had causes enough for complaint
against the Duke — the taxation he had burdened
them with, the misgovernment he had allowed, the
favour he had shown the English ; but they at least
preferred him to the Armagnacs, of whom Charles
was now the head. Paris rejected Charles, scornfully
calling him the *soi-disant* Dauphin, thus casting on
his legitimacy a doubt which Isabeau's conduct had
too well warranted. The new Duke of Burgundy,
Philip the Good, saw in the English his father's
avengers, and acknowledged Henry's right to the
throne. By the treaty of Troyes (1420), the King of
England was appointed Regent of France for the
lifetime of Charles VI., the succession was assured to
him and his heirs, and the Princess Catherine was
given him in marriage. The mad King, a pitiful
puppet in any hands, signed the treaty, which
Isabeau had furthered with all her might, caring

nothing that it disinherited her son, and more than hinted at her own dishonour. In the following year it was confirmed by the States-General, convened at Paris.

In the midst of his triumphs, the King of England died at Vincennes (1422). He had just taken Meaux, and it was during the siege that news came to him of his son's birth at Windsor. "Henry of Monmouth," he said with prophetic sadness, "will have conquered much in a short reign. Henry of Windsor will reign long and lose all."

The King of France outlived him only a few weeks. The people, especially the poorest of them, mourned for him unfeignedly. His very misery had endeared him to them. "Alas! dear Prince," they lamented, "thou hast gone to rest; we are left in tribulation and pain." When his coffin was lowered into the grave at St Denis, the French King-at-arms, breaking his staff over it, cried aloud, "God have mercy on the soul of the very noble and excellent Prince Charles, King of France, sixth of the name, our *natural* and sovereign lord!" And then, "God grant long life to Henry, King of France and England, our sovereign lord!"

France was divided between two Kings. The baby monarch of England was acknowledged by the northern provinces, with the exception of a few scattered towns; by Guienne, Gascony, and the states of Brittany and Burgundy. The country immediately south of the Loire, with Saintonge, Quercy, and Dauphiné, were true to their "natural lord," Charles VII., who was recognised also by the royal vassals south of the Garonne and those of the Mediterranean provinces.

He was just twenty years old, a well-grown handsome young Prince, good-natured, lazy, fond of pleasure, fond of favourites; yet neither giving nor gaining much affection, for with his carelessness he combined utter coldness of heart. He seemed born to lose, not to win back, a kingdom. Generally he held his little court at Bourges, where he lived as gaily as fate would permit, sometimes in want of the veriest necessaries, sometimes faring luxuriously, and lavishing on follies the subsidies that should have been spent in recovering his birthright. Meagre supplies, wrung from a wretched and famished people, were voted him by his States-General, which met now at Poitiers, now at Carcassonne or Beziers. His troops were for the most part Gascons, Lombards, or Scotch, who got no pay, and therefore were under no control, but lived by pillage.

Henry had left the regency of his two kingdoms to his brothers, the Dukes of Bedford and Gloucester, committing France, as the more difficult charge, to Bedford, who was the older and wiser. Bedford's first care was to strengthen his alliance with the

Duke of Burgundy, without whose help he could not hope to keep any mastery in France. He married, in 1423, Philip's younger sister, the elder being at the same time given to Arthur of Richmond, brother of the Duke of Brittany.

Before attempting to drive Charles out of central France, Bedford resolved to take those places north of the Loire which gave shelter to his partisans. The French party lost one town after another, and in 1424 suffered a great defeat at Verneuil, where the Scotch troops of Charles were nearly all killed. The English gave no quarter to those born enemies of theirs; the south-French, who were jealous of them, gave them no support. It was even said that their destruction half consoled the Armagnac captains for the loss of the battle.

But the Duke of Gloucester's folly came near thwarting all Bedford's plans. Philip of Burgundy had married his cousin, the Duke of Brabant, a weak and sickly youth, to Jacqueline, Countess in her own right of Holland and Hainault, hoping that the union would prove childless, and that he himself might inherit the estates of both wife and husband. Jacqueline, a beautiful and self-willed woman, soon grew tired of her uncongenial lord. She fled to England, and having persuaded the anti-Pope Benedict to grant her a divorce, offered herself to Gloucester, who married her, and went with her to take possession of her inheritance. A tedious war followed, in which the Duke of Burgundy took his cousin's part; but Pope Martin V. annulled Jacqueline's self-arranged marriage, and Gloucester, after some blustering, returned home, leaving the lady to continue the struggle on her own account.

The coolness between England and Burgundy gave new hope to the National party, of which Yolande of Anjou, the King's mother-in-law, was the truest and warmest adherent. She did much to wean Charles from the Armagnacs, and persuaded him to make friends with Richmond, and give him the office of Constable. Richmond, a rough Breton, and no courtier, had the Armagnacs banished from the King's person, and put to death two of the favourites who had dared to oppose him. In their stead, he gave the King a favourite of his own choosing, George de la Trémouille, who was no sooner installed at Court than he turned against his late patron, and prevailed on Charles to banish him. Thus was thrown away a chance of reconciliation with Burgundy.

The Duke of Brittany, who for a while had acknowledged Charles, now did homage to Henry (1428). The Duke of Burgundy returned to his alliance with England. The cause of Charles seemed lost, and lost mainly by his own negligence and folly. The " King of Bourges," as the Parisians had nicknamed him, meditated leaving the central provinces to their fate, and retiring into Dauphiné. He had no thought of going forward to meet his enemies, and the time had come for them to carry the war southward, and conquer France beyond the Loire. The Earl of Salisbury had orders to lay siege to Orleans.

Orleans, "the Key of the South," formed a sort of irregular square on the north bank of the Loire, in the Beauce. It was strongly walled, and had five outlets : the Paris and Bernier gates on the north, the Burgundy gate on the east, the Renart gate on the west ; the fifth gate opened upon a bridge of seventeen arches, some of which rested on an island which has since disappeared. Over this island was a fort called the Bastile St. Antoine, and at its southern abutment the bridge was guarded by another fort called the Tourelles and a strong boulevard. The burgesses bestowed much care on their fortifications, and devoted two-thirds of the municipal revenue to keeping them up.

Orleans was not all comprised within its walls. Beyond them stretched suburbs, "the most beautiful in France," which the citizens now burned down, that they should not shelter the enemy. The people prepared for the defence with great devotion and lightness of heart. They had repulsed Henry V. in 1421, and the recollection was an encouraging one. Everybody, monks, students, women even, worked at the fortifications. The city was well off for provisions

B

and war-stores ; other towns sent in large contributions, for all France knew that the fall of Orleans would probably mean the loss of the whole kingdom.

It was an ancient privilege of the place to be defended only by its own citizens, but now they gladly welcomed all who came to help them. Raoul de Gaucourt, who had bravely defended Harfleur, was their governor. Their Duke, who had been made prisoner at Agincourt, was represented by his illegitimate brother John, Count of Dunois. La Hire, Saintrailles, and many other captains, came with their troops to reinforce the garrison.

Before attacking Orleans, Salisbury took several important places on his road thither, and in its neighbourhood. It was not until he had secured Meun and Baugency, Châteauneuf and Jargeau, that he crossed the Loire, took Olivet, a little south of Orleans, and established himself in the Augustin convent, just beyond the Tourelles. It had been set on fire at his approach, but his men repaired and fortified the ruins. He intended first to get possession of the bridge, and so cut off the besieged from the southern provinces ; then, to take the city by storm.

On October 21st, he attacked the Tourelles, and in two days forced their defenders to retire to the Bastile St. Antoine, for the better protection of which had been built a wooden fort called the Boulevard de la Belle Croix. Between this new bulwark and the bastile the besieged now broke away one arch of the bridge, laying a movable bridge over the gap. On the 24th, Salisbury entered the Tourelles, and destroyed the two arches of the bridge nearest to them. That evening he was viewing Orleans from a loophole of the fort, when a splinter from a cannon-stone, fired at a venture, so the story goes, by a child within the city, struck him in the forehead. In three days he died, and most of his army retired to await reinforcements and a new general. The Tourelles and the Augustins were left in charge of Sir William Glasdale.

It was not until the end of December that 2500 English, led by the Earl of Suffolk, who had been appointed in Salisbury's place, Scales, Talbot, and other famous commanders, appeared on the west of Orleans, and took possession of the ruined church of St. Laurence, close to the river. On the opposite shore they built the boulevard of St. Privé, and on the island of Charlemagne, between the two, another boulevard. Suffolk then re-crossed the stream, and built a boulevard at the Croix Boissée, opposite the Renart gate. His plan was to surround the city with forts, so as to cut off supplies, and starve it into submission.

Early in February, 1429, the besieged learned that Falstaff was coming from Paris with a great train of provisions, which the Count of Clermont and other partisans of Charles had determined to intercept. Accordingly, fifteen hundred men, led by the best knights in Orleans, went out to aid in the enterprise. Near Rouvray they saw Clermont's troops in the distance, and came upon Falstaff's waggons, which were protected by about seventeen hundred men-at-arms. They sent to the Count for orders, and he bade then wait on horseback until he should join them. Falstaff profited by this delay, and drew up his men behind the waggons and a hedge of those pointed stakes which the English troops always carried with them. The men of Orleans grew impatient, and they and some of ·Clermont's Scotch soldiers who had ridden up to them dismounted and attacked the barricade. They were driven back by a shower of arrows, and then Falstaff sent out his cavalry, which easily routed them, unhorsed as they were, and encumbered by their heavy armour. Clermont never came to their aid, but watched from a distance the thorough defeat of the men who had acted against his orders, and then rode on to Orleans with his useless army. This skirmish was called the Battle of the Herrings, because several of the waggons were laden with barrels of salt fish as a provision for Lent.

The National party was greatly discouraged. The fall of Orleans was believed inevitable, and now its own bishop, with Regnault de Chartres, Archbishop of Reims and Chancellor of the kingdom, deserted it, rat-like, in the day of its trouble. The Count of Clermont went away also, carrying his reinforcements with him.

La Hire was sent to Chinon, where the King was, to entreat him for help, but the King, himself in a desperate condition, could do nothing for his loyal city. The English continued to hem it in. In spite of the frequent sorties of the garrison, they built a bastile at St. Loup, on its eastern side, and on its north-west two great boulevards, which they called London and Rouen. In mid-April they completed a great bastile further to the north, and named it Paris.

Hitherto the besieged had contrived occasionally to get supplies from without, but now, as fort after fort rose up about their walls, it became evident that their reduction by famine was only a matter of time. In their distress they had sent deputies to Philip of Burgundy, begging him, as the near relation of their Duke, to protect his domain from the English. Philip would gladly have undertaken the charge, and so established his power in the heart of France, but the Regent's consent had to be asked, and he bluntly refused it, saying " he would be sorry to have beaten the bush that others might catch the game." The offended Duke declared that he would no longer help to do an injustice, and recalled his troops that were with the besieging army (April 17th). Three days later the English completed a bastile at St. Jean-le-Blanc, on the southern bank of the river, a little above the city.

By that time the deputies had returned from their successless errand, but the people's sorrow at their failure was lost in the gladness of a new hope. They had looked to the King and to the Duke for help, and found none, but now they had tidings of a deliverance greater than duke or king could give. Clermont and his men-of-war had failed them; the Church, in the person of her prelates, had forsaken them: but Heaven had interfered while there was yet time. Joan of Arc, sent by God, led by the saints, was on her way to save Orleans.

CHAPTER II.

THE MISSION.

ON the 6th of January, 1412, Jeanne d'Arc, or, as we in England call her, Joan of Arc, was born at Domremy, a little village on the left bank of the Meuse, on land bordering upon Lorraine, but belonging to the French crown. Her parents, Jacques d'Arc and Isabelle Romée, were simple peasants, " of good life and reputation," who brought up their children to work hard, fear God, and honour the saints. Beside Joan, they had four children—three sons, Jacques, Jean, and Pierre, and a daughter, Catherine.

Joan's native valley was fair and fertile. The low hills that bounded it were covered with thick forests, and the rich meadows along the Meuse were gay with flowers, which gave to the chief town in the district its name of Vaucouleurs, *Vallis colorum.* Domremy, built on a slope, touched upon those flowery meadows, but over the hill behind it spread an ancient oak-wood, the *Bois Chesnu* of legend and prophecy. Between the forest and the village rose solitary a

great beech, "beautiful as a lily," about which the
country people told a thousand tales.   They called it
the "Fairies' Tree," the "Tree of the Ladies," the
"Beautiful May."   In old times the fairies had danced
round it, and under its shadow a noble knight had
formerly dared to meet and talk with an elfin lady.
But now, in Joan's time, the presence of the fairies
was less certain, for the priest of Domremy came once
a-year to say mass under the tree, and exorcise it and
a spring that bubbled up close by.   On festival days
the young villagers hung it with garlands, danced and
played round it, and rested under its boughs to eat
certain cakes which their mothers had made for them.
During her childhood, Joan brought her cakes and
garlands like the rest, danced with them, and sang
more than she danced ; but as she grew older, she
would steal away and carry her flowers to the neigh-
bouring chapel of Our Lady of Domremy.

Her early years were, considering the times, quiet
and peaceful.   With the war raging to its west and
north, Domremy had comparatively little to do.   The
villagers were Armagnac and loyal, all but one man,
whose head, so Joan afterwards avowed, she would
willingly have seen cut off, "had it been the will of
God."   At Maxey, just across the Meuse, the people
were as eagerly Burgundian, and between the boys of
the two villages there were frequent fights, from which
Joan's brothers would return bruised and bleeding.

The Burgundians disturbed Domremy just enough to keep alive there a hatred of them, and still more of their friends the English. Once the villagers fled in terror to Neufchâteau, and returned to find their homes pillaged and burned by Burgundian partisans. Often, when Burgundian soldiers were seen in the distance, the flocks and herds were hurriedly taken to a fortified island in the river. News of English successes, of French defeats, and the sorrows of the French King, were brought by fugitives from the war, by travelling monks, and other wanderers. Joan helped to receive those wayfarers, waited 'on them, gave up her own bed to them sometimes ; and what they told of the woes of France she heard with intense sympathy, and pondered in her heart.

Her bringing-up fitted her for the tender fulfilling of all womanly duties. Unlike most girls of her class, she had few out-door tasks, but spent most of her time at her mother's side, doing the work of the house, learning to sew and spin, to repeat the Belief, the Ave Mary, and the legends of the saints. Her work done, her dearest pleasure was to go to the village church, which was close to her father's cottage, and there kneel in prayer, gaze on the pictured saints and angels, or listen to the bells calling the faithful to worship : she had always a peculiar delight in the sound of church bells. She fasted regularly, and went often to confession ; so often, that her young com-

panions were inclined to jest at her devotion, and
even her chosen friends, Haumette and Mengette,
half-scolded her for being over-religious. But her
faith bore sound fruit. The little money she got she
gave in alms. She nursed the sick, she was gentle to
the young and weak, obedient to her parents, kind to
all. " There was no one like her in the village," said
her priest. " She was a good girl," testified an old
peasant—" such a daughter as I would gladly have
had." A good girl, indeed : they were pure and
helpful hands that for a while held the fate of
France.

There was a prophecy current during that unhappy
time—an old prophecy of Merlin—which the suffering
people had taken and applied to their own day and
their own need. " The kingdom, lost by a woman,
was to be saved by a woman." The woman who had
lost it was Isabeau, the wicked queen, the false wife,
the unnatural mother. Who was she that should
save it ? In the east of France it was said that the
deliverer would be a maid from the marshes of Lorraine. Joan knew the ancient prophecy, and in her
young mind it became blended with legends of the
saints, with stories of Bible heroines, with her own
ardent faith and high aspirations. She loved more
and more to be alone. Night and day the wonderful
child brooded on the sorrows of France. She sent
out her vague hopes and yearnings in tears and

prayers, and passionate thoughts that *were* prayers, and they all came back to her with form and sound, in the visions and voices that were henceforth to be the rulers of her life.

They came first when she was thirteen years old. On a summer's day, at noon, she was in her father's garden, when suddenly by the church there appeared a great light, and out of the light a *voice* spoke to her—" Joan, be a good child ; go often to church." She was frightened then, but both voice and brightness came again and again, and grew dear and familiar. Noble shapes appeared in the glory. St. Michael showed himself to her ; St. Catherine and St. Margaret bent over her their crowned and radiant heads, bidding her " be good ; trust in God." They told her of " the sorrow there was in the kingdom of France," and warned her that one day it would be her mission to go and carry help to the King. While to outward eyes she lived as usual, she had a life apart, given to God and her saints. She vowed her virginity to Heaven, but of her vow and the visions that had led her to it she told no one, not even the priest who confessed her. Her meditations, her prayers and unearthly friendships, made of her no sickly dreamer nor hot-brained fanatic. She grew up strong, tall, and handsome, with a healthy mind in her healthy body.

Meanwhile the dangers of France darkened and thickened. The Regent was pushing the war southward; Salisbury was on his way to Orleans; the "King of Bourges," poor, indolent, ill-advised, was deliberating whether he should retreat into Dauphiné, or Spain, or Scotland. Joan's voices grew more frequent and more urgent. Their word now was always, "Go—go into France!" At last they had told her the way—"Go to Vaucouleurs, to Robert de Baudricourt, the governor; he will give you men-at-arms, and send you to the King." It was now that Joan's trial began. While her beautiful visitors had spoken vaguely of some "deliverance" she was to bring about in the future, she had listened with trembling joy, with wild impatience to begin her mission. But now they had plainly shown her the distasteful first step, and for a moment she shrank from taking it. How could a peasant brave the governor of Vaucouleurs? How was a modest girl to venture among rude men-at-arms? How could a dutiful child leave her parents and her home? "Alas!" she pleaded, "I am a poor girl; I know neither how to ride nor how to fight." She had a short, hard struggle with her own weakness, but the voices did not alter, and she set herself to do their bidding.

Her uncle, Durant Laxart, with whom she evidently was a favourite, lived at Burey, a village near Vaucouleurs, and in May, 1428, she went to his house for a visit. After a few days she confided to him something of her plans, reminding him of the old prophecy of Merlin, but never speaking of her visions. With much difficulty she prevailed on him to help her. He went with her to Vaucouleurs, and before the governor, to whom she made known her errand. " Send and tell the Dauphin," she said, " to wait and not offer battle to his enemies, because God will give him help before mid-Lent. The kingdom belongs not to the Dauphin, but to my Lord ; but my Lord wills that the Dauphin shall be King, and hold it in trust. In spite of his enemies he shall be King, and I myself shall lead him to be crowned." " And who is your lord ?" demanded Baudricourt. She answered, " The King of Heaven." The governor, a rough and practical soldier, laughed at the young peasant in her coarse red dress, and bade her uncle chastise her well, and take her home to her father.

She returned to Domremy with her heart more than ever fixed on the work she had before her. Now and again she let fall words that revealed enough to make her parents anxious and fearful. Her father dreamed that she had gone away with the soldiers. " If I thought such a thing could happen," he said to her brothers, " I would bid you drown her, and if you refused, I would drown her myself." But she was of a marriageable age : why should she not marry, stay at home, and bring up children, like other women ? A lover came forward, a bold one, who, when she rejected him, summoned her before the court at Toul, declaring that she had promised to be his wife. But she went before the judges, spoke out bravely, and defeated her persevering suitor.

As the months passed, her longing increased to be gone and do her voices' bidding. Once more she obtained her uncle's help. His wife was ill, and he came to Domremy and got leave for Joan to go back with him and nurse her. She went, keeping secret the real end of her journey. " If I had had a hundred fathers and a hundred mothers," she said later, " and if I had been a king's daughter, I should have gone." She took leave of her companion Mengette, but to Haumette, her dearer friend, she would not trust herself to say farewell. Her uncle took her to Vaucouleurs, and gave her in charge of a wheelwright's wife, Catherine Royer, with whom she lived for some weeks. She went constantly to mass, she helped her hostess in the house, and was gentle and obedient as a young maiden should be. At the same time, she spoke frankly of her mission to any who chose to hear.

She again went to the governor, who received her no better than before. But she was not cast down. " I must go to the Dauphin," she said, " though I should go on my knees." Many people went to see her, among others a brave gentleman of Metz, Jean de Novelonpont. " What are you doing here, my child ?" he asked her, jestingly. " Shall the King be driven out of France, and must we all turn English ?" " I am come to this royal city," she answered, " to bid Robert de Baudricourt take or send me to the King, but he does not heed my words ; and yet before mid-Lent I must be before the King, though I should wear away my legs to the knees. For no one else in the world, neither kings, nor dukes, nor the daughter of the King of Scotland,[1] can recover the kingdom of France, and there is no help but in me. And indeed I would rather spin with my poor mother, for this is not my calling ; but I must go and do it, for it is my Lord's will." Like Baudricourt, the knight asked her, " Who is your lord ?" and she answered, " He is God." But, unlike Baudricourt, he was touched by her words. In the old feudal fashion, he laid his hands within hers and vowed that by God's help he would take her to the King. Another worthy gentle-man, Bertrand de Poulengy, gave a like promise.

Baudricourt was now forced to listen to Joan. The people of Vaucouleurs believed in her with the ready faith of that time, and she had at least two of his own class to take her part. But those voices of hers, were they of God or of the Devil ? Was she witch or saint ? The governor, like many another good

---

[1] It had been proposed that Louis, son of Charles VII., should marry Margaret, daughter of James I. of Scotland. The marriage took place in 1436.

soldier, had some weakness of superstition. He went
to see her, taking with him a priest, who began to
exorcise her, bidding her avaunt if she were of the
Evil One. Joan approached the priest and knelt
before him, honouring not him, but his office : for, as
she said afterwards, he had not done well; he had
heard her confess, and should have known that no
evil spirit spoke by her.

While she was waiting Baudricourt's pleasure, the
Duke of Lorraine, who was ill at Nancy, heard of her,
and, hoping for the revelation of some cure, desired to
see her. He sent her a safe-conduct, and she went to
Nancy under care of her uncle. But she knew only
what her *voices* taught her, and she had no power to
cure any ills but those of France. This she told the
Duke, promising him her prayers, and begging him to
aid in her enterprise. He sent her back honourably,
but did not pledge himself to the royal cause.

The people of Vaucouleurs came forward to help
Joan. They gave her a horse, and the dress and
equipment of a soldier ; for as she was to travel with
men, she wisely chose to wear man's attire. Baudricourt still doubted and delayed. The people she was
sojourning with pitied her anxiety. " The time was
long to her as to a woman in travail," Catherine
Royer said. On the day of the battle of Rouvray
she went to the governor. " In God's name," she
said, " you are too slow about sending me. To-day

the Dauphin has suffered great loss near Orleans, and he is in danger of yet greater if you do not send me to him soon." At last he yielded to her urgency. He gave her a sword and a letter to the King, and let her prepare to depart. Bertrand de Poulengy, Jean de Novelonpont, and four armed men of lesser rank were to accompany her. She did not see her parents to bid them farewell, but she sent them a letter, entreating them to pardon her. She spoke cheerily to those who were afraid for her safety. God and "her brothers of Paradise" would guard her and her little escort on their dangerous journey. On February 23rd, 1429, they set out, Baudricourt bidding her " Go, come of it what may."

Her most timid well-wisher could hardly have exaggerated the perils of the journey. More than half of it was through the enemy's country, where there was continual risk of being stopped and questioned. The rivers, swollen by the winter rains, were unfordable ; therefore the travellers had to cross over bridges in full sight of fortified towns. In the daring of her faith, Joan would have ridden forward boldly and waited to hear mass in every village on the road, but her guides had more worldly prudence. They insisted on travelling chiefly at night, and in the day-time rested in some unfrequented spot, where she lay down among them and slept, guarded by her own purity and the influence she had already won over them.

c

Having crossed the Loire at Gien, they found themselves in the King's country, where they could travel openly and declare the cause of their journey. From Gien the news went to Orleans that a shepherd-maid had passed, whose mission it was to deliver the city and lead Charles to be crowned, and the Orleanists at once sent envoys to Chinon to make inquiries about Joan, and entreat the King not to neglect this chance for their relief. On the eleventh day of their journey the Maid and her party reached St. Catherine de Fierbois, near Chinon, where they rested, and Joan heard three masses. She sent a letter to Charles requesting an audience, and telling him she had come a hundred and fifty leagues to help him. The next day, March 6th, she rode on to Chinon.

An interview with Charles was no such simple affair as she had fancied. Between her and him were doubts, jealousies, intrigues. La Tremouille, who, rather than lose his power over the King, would have let the kingdom go to destruction, was her enemy before he saw her. The Archbishop of Reims, that wary diplomatist, and many of the King's most trusted councillors, were against her. But Queen Yolande and the many who hated and despised La Tremouille were on her side. Jean de Novelonpont and Bertrand de Poulengy spoke warmly in her favour. Her friends prevailed, and after two days' waiting she was admitted to the castle. As she was passing through the gate, a man-at-arms called out, "What, is that the Maid?" and added a coarse jest and an oath. Joan turned and looked gravely at him. "Alas!" she said, "you blaspheme God, and you are so near your death!" Within an hour the man was drowned by accident, and those words of hers were repeated far and wide as a proof of her prophetic power.

The Count of Vendôme led her into the royal presence. She entered meekly, but undismayed; in her visions she had seen finer company than any earthly court could show her. Charles stood among the crowd of nobles, and when she knelt before him he pointed to a richly-dressed lord, saying, "That is the King, not I." But she knew the King, probably from descriptions she had heard of him, and answered, "In God's name, gracious Prince, you are he, and none other." She then repeated to him the words which, like a charm, had brought her so far and overcome so much: "I am Joan the Maid, sent by God to save France," and she asked him for troops, that she might go and raise the siege of Orleans. Presently the Duke of Alençon came in, and the King having told her who he was, she bade him welcome. "The more there are of the blood-royal of France," she said, "the better it will be." Alençon, who had lately returned from a three years' captivity in England, and was still paying a ruinous ransom, sympathised with the girl-champion, and was inclined to believe in her.

The King and his advisers went cautiously to work. They sent two monks to Domremy to inquire into Joan's character and past life. They called her now and again to Court, where statesmen and churchmen questioned her closely. Meanwhile, she was honourably treated. She was given to the charge of Bellier, the King's lieutenant, whose wife was a lady of virtue and piety, and many distinguished persons visited her at the castle of Courdray, where she was lodged. One day she rode with the lance before the King, and acquitted herself so well that the Duke of Alençon rewarded her with the gift of a beautiful horse. Could she have at all forgotten her mission, the time would have passed pleasantly; as it was, she wearied for action.

At last she sought the King, and said to him, " Gracious Dauphin"—until Charles was anointed at Reims with the sacred oil, he was no real King in her eyes—" Gracious Dauphin, why will you not believe me ? I tell you, God has pity on you, your kingdom and people, for St. Louis and St. Charlemagne are on their knees before Him praying for you." She then took him apart, and told him a secret of great importance, which made his face to " beam with joy." Joan never revealed what she had said to the King, but he himself confided it to his young chamberlain, the Lord of Boisy, who told it long afterwards. Some days before Joan's arrival, Charles, despairing of help, doubting, as the son of Isabeau might doubt, his right to the crown, had knelt alone in his oratory, and prayed silently that if he were the true heir, the real son of the King, to whom the kingdom really belonged, it would please God to keep and defend him in it; but if not, that God would suffer him to escape death and prison, and let him find refuge in Spain or Scotland. Now, Joan's words came as an answer to his prayer and his fears—" I tell you from my Lord that you are the true heir of France and the son of the King."

To satisfy all doubts about Joan, it was settled that she should be taken to Poitiers, where the Parliament was assembled, and be there questioned by a royal commission. " In God's name, let us go," she said ; " I shall have hard work, but my Lord will help me." She was lodged in the house of Jean Rabateau, advocate-general to the Parliament, and committed to his wife's care. The Archbishop of Reims called together churchmen and learned doctors, among whom were Gerard Machet, the King's confessor ; the Bishops of Poitiers and Maguelonne, Guillaume Aymeri, and the Dominican Seguin, from whom we have the best account of the proceedings, the official report of which was lost before Joan's great trial at

Rouen. The Commissioners met at Rabateau's house, and having called Joan, showed her "by good and fair arguments" that she was unworthy of belief. They reasoned with her for more than two hours, and she answered them so well that they were greatly amazed. In spite of their expressed distrust, she spoke to them freely and fully, told how her voices had bidden her go into France, how she had wept at their command and yet obeyed it, how she had come safely, because she was doing the will of God.

"You require an army," said Guillaume Aymeri, "saying it is God's will that the English shall quit France. If that be so, there is no need for men-at-arms, because God can drive them away by His pleasure." "The men-at-arms shall fight," she answered, "and God shall give the victory;" and the monk confessed that she had answered well.

Seguin, "a very sour man," a native of Limousin, inquired in what language her voices spoke. "A better language than yours," she replied sharply. The offended provincial then asked what *sign* she had to show. "I am not come to give signs," she said. "Take me to Orleans, and I will show you the sign I am sent for." When the examination had dragged on for three weeks, two of the doctors came one day to question her, bringing with them Gobert Thibaut, the King's equerry, whom she had known at Chinon. She clapped him, comrade-like, on the shoulder,

exclaiming, "Would that I had many more men of as
good will as you!" Then turning to the doctors, she
said, " I believe you are come to catechise me. Listen!—I know neither A nor B, but there is more in
God's books than in yours. He has sent me to save
Orleans and crown the King." She demanded paper
and ink. "Write what I tell you!" she said, and
dictated to the amazed scholars the famous letter
which soon after was sent to the English.

The grave and stern commissioners were won by
the faith, the boldness, and the simplicity of the young
peasant. None of them, not even the "sour monk"
Seguin, bore her any grudge for the occasional sharp-
ness of her replies. Many of them believed firmly
that she was inspired, and quoted the old prophecy of
Merlin, and the recent visions of Marie of Avignon,
the seer, who had foretold the coming of a maid who
should deliver France. All of them trusted in her
good faith, and appreciated more or less the influence
she would have over the people. They advised,
almost commanded, Charles to employ her. Her life,
they said, has been carefully inquired into; for six
weeks she has been kept near the King; persons of
all ranks, men and women, have seen and talked with
her, and have found in her only "goodness, humility,
chastity, devotion, seemliness, and simplicity." She
has promised to show her *sign* before Orleans: let the
King send her there, for to reject her would be to

reject the Holy Spirit and render himself unworthy of divine help.

Besides her learned judges, she had others whom, had she been an impostor, she would have found hard to deceive. Keen women's eyes had been set to watch her, and had seen no fault in her. Her hostesses at Chinon and Poitiers bore witness to her discretion and piety. Queen Yolande and other honourable matrons declared her worthy of her name—Joan the Maid. The ladies who came to see the warrior-damsel were amazed to find her a mere girl, "very simple, and speaking little." Her goodness and innocence moved them to tears. She prayed them to pardon her for the man's attire she wore ; but in that lawless day the most modest women must have well understood that such a dress was fittest and safest for her who had to live among men.

Towards the end of April she was sent to Tours, where a military staff was appointed her. Jean d'Aulon, a brave and honest gentleman, was made the chief of her household. Jean de Novelonpont and Bertrand de Poulengy remained with her. Louis de Contes, whom she had known at Courdray, and a youth named Raimond, were her pages. Two heralds were given to her, and Jean Pasquerel became her almoner. Her brothers Jean and Pierre, who had followed her, were included in her retinue. A suit of beautiful armour was made for her. She was provided

with a banner after her own device—white,embroidered
with lilies: on one side of it, a picture of God enthroned
on clouds and holding a globe in His hand ; on the
other, the shield of France, supported by two angels.
She had also a pennon, whereon was represented the
Annunciation. The King would have given her a
sword, but her voices, she said, had told her of the
only one she might use, an ancient weapon with five
crosses on its blade, which was lying buried behind
the altar in the church of St. Catherine de Fierbois.
A messenger was sent, and in the place she had told
of was found an old rusty sword such as she had
described. After being polished, it was brought to
her with two rich scabbards, one of crimson velvet,
the other of cloth of gold ; but the practical Maid got
herself yet another of strong leather for daily wear.

CHAPTER III.

ORLEANS.

JOAN being accepted, the National party made rapid preparations for the relief of Orleans. Queen Yolande and the Duke of Alençon went to Blois to hasten the collecting of troops and supplies, and Joan soon followed them, accompanied by the Archbishop of Reims. Before long an army of about 6000 men was got together. It was commanded by the best Armagnac captains, the Marshal de Boussac, the Sire de Retz, La Hire, Florent d'Illiers, Poton de Saintrailles, and others—strange comrades, most of them, for the pure Maid with her white banner and sacred sword.

Her first care was that the army given her by God should be worthy of His favour. For the priests attached to it, she had a banner made with a picture of the Crucifixion, beneath which they said mass and sang hymns to the Virgin morning and evening. She entreated her soldiers to confess themselves, and banished from their camp the women of ill fame who would have followed it.

Before leaving Blois, she sent to the besiegers of Orleans the letter she had dictated at Poitiers :—

+ JESUS MARIA. +

" King of England, and you Duke of Bedford who call yourself Regent of France ; William de la Pole, Earl of Suffolk ; and you Thomas Lord Scales, who style yourselves lieutenants of the said Bedford, do right to the King of Heaven. Render to the Maid who is sent by God the keys of all the good towns you have taken and violated in France. She is sent hither by God to restore the blood royal. She is very ready to make peace if you will do her right by giving up France and paying for what you have held. And you archers, companions of war, noble and otherwise, who are before the good city of Orleans, begone into your own land in God's name, or expect news from the Maid who will shortly go to see you to your very great hurt. King of England, if you do not so, I am chief of war, and wherever I shall find your people in France I will drive them out, willing or not willing, and if they do not obey I will slay them all, but if they obey, I will have them to mercy. I am come hither by God, the King of Heaven, body for body, to put you out of France, in spite of those who would work treason and mischief against the kingdom. Think not you shall ever hold the kingdom from the King of Heaven, the Son of the blessed Mary ; King Charles shall hold it, for God wills it so, and has revealed it to him by the Maid. If you believe not the news sent by God through the Maid, wherever we shall meet you we will strike boldly, and make such a noise as has not been in France these thousand years. Be sure that God can send more strength to the Maid than you can bring to any assault against her and her good men-at-arms ; and then we shall see who has the better right, the King of Heaven or you. Duke of Bedford, the Maid prays you not to bring about your own destruction. If you do her right, you may yet go in her company where the French shall do the finest deed that has ever been done in Christendom, and if you do not, you shall be reminded shortly of your great wrongs."

The captains before Orleans read this letter with mingled scorn and fury, and found no name too insulting for the upstart peasant who had dared to defy the majesty of England. In violation of the laws of war, they kept her herald, threatening to burn him, and only put off doing so until they should have consulted the University of Paris.

On Thursday, April 28th, the relieving army set out from Blois, the priests going before and singing the *Veni Creator* round their banner of the Cross. Joan wished to march along the north bank of the Loire, and through the line of English forts ; her voices, she said, had told her that the convoy would pass them without hurt. But the captains, who had little faith in her revelations, preferred keeping the river between themselves and the chief bastiles of the enemy. They had orders, however, to obey the Maid, so, to avoid contradicting her, they misled her as to the position of Orleans ; crossing the bridge at Blois, they advanced by the south bank of the stream, through the Sologne. When night came, the army encamped on the plain, and Joan, who lay down in her armour, arose bruised and weary for the next day's march. But all her fatigue was forgotten when she reached Olivet and saw how she had been deceived. She would at once have attacked the bastile of St. Jean-le-Blanc, but she was overruled, and the army went on to a point opposite Chécy, two leagues above Orleans.

Dunois, with a following of knights and citizens, came up the river to welcome the convoy. When he approached Joan, she asked him, " Are you the bastard of Orleans ?" " Yes," he replied, " and I am glad of your coming." "And did you advise that I should be brought by this side of the river, and not straight to Talbot and the English ?" He answered that it was so, he and the council having judged it safest. " In God's name," she said, " my Lord's counsel is safer and wiser than yours. You thought to deceive me, but you have deceived yourselves, for I bring you the best help that ever knight or city had ; for it is God's help, not sent for love of me, but by God's pleasure. At the prayer of St. Louis and St. Charlemagne He has had pity on Orleans, and will not suffer the enemy to have both the Duke of Orleans and his city."

The supplies could only be conveyed to Orleans by

boats, which, the wind being contrary, could not sail up the river to fetch them. Dunois and the rest now saw how great had been their mistake. But presently the wind changed and the boats arrived. The little fleet, having been loaded with provisions and cattle, returned and discharged its cargo, while the besieged, to divert the attention of the English, attacked their bastile of St. Loup. The question now was, how to take the army over. Dunois and the captains advised Joan to enter Orleans herself, but to let the troops return to Blois, cross the river there, and join her as speedily as possible. It was with difficulty that she consented. Her men, she said, were prepared for the work, "confessed, penitent, and of good will;" with them she did not fear all the power of England. She left the priests with them, and with La Hire, Dunois, and two hundred lances, went down the river to Orleans.

At eight that evening she entered by the Burgundy gate, riding a white horse, her standard carried before her. The people thronged to meet her, wild with joy, "as if she had been an angel of God." " They felt comforted and, as it were, *dis-besieged* by the divine virtue there was said to be in that simple Maid." They crowded so upon her, that one of their torches set fire to the border of her standard, and when she bent forward and crushed out the flame, the little brave action seemed a miracle to the excited multitude. After returning thanks to God in the cathedral, she rode to the house of Jacques Boucher, treasurer to the Duke of Orleans, and was hospitably received by his wife and his young daughter Charlotte, whom she took to share her chamber during her stay in the city.

She would have begun the attack next day, but most of the leaders decided to wait until the army should have returned from Blois. La Hire and Florent d'Illiers, however, led a sally on their own account, but were repulsed. Among the bold Armagnacs, La Hire was one of the boldest and most lawless. For him, might was right. "If God were to turn man-at-arms," he used to say, "He would be a freebooter;" and his prayer before a pillaging expedition was, "Good Lord, I pray Thee, deal with La Hire as he would deal with Thee were he God and wert Thou La Hire." This jovial brigand, whose every other word was a blasphemy, took a liking to Joan, and for her sake gave up swearing for a while, except "by his staff," the one oath she allowed him.

That day she sent two heralds with a letter to the English, summoning them to raise the siege and restore her first messenger. At the same time, Dunois sent them word that, unless the heralds returned in safety, he would kill all his English prisoners. They still detained one, Guyenne, but let the others go, with an insulting message to the Maid, threatening that she should yet be burnt, and bidding her "go back to her cow-keeping." This did not prevent her from making an appeal to them in person. That evening she went up into the Belle Croix fort, and summoned Glasdale to surrender; whereupon he and his officers answered her, as she might have expected, with scorn and reviling.

Next morning, Sunday, May 1st, Dunois went to fetch the army from Blois. The Maid rode with him a little way, and he and his following passed unmolested by the English forts. The days of his absence were spent by Joan in making friends with the citizens, in attending mass and riding out to reconnoitre the enemy's siege-works. The enthusiastic people followed her everywhere, fearing nothing so long as they were near her. On Tuesday some reinforcements arrived, and news came that the army was on its way.

It was well that Dunois had gone to hasten its coming, for when he reached Blois he found Regnault de Chartres and the King's other lukewarm advisers debating whether it should go back to Orleans at all. Most of the captains, however, were eager for the expedition, Dunois' arguments turned the scale, and the troops, with a new supply of stores, were suffered to depart. This time they took the northern side of the river, and on May 4th Joan went a league out of the city to meet them. The whole army passed the line of forts and entered Orleans. The besiegers made no sign, and it is not wonderful that the English soldiers, seeing that strange apathy of their leaders, believed Joan to be a witch, whose arts it would be useless to resist.

The same day, Dunois told her that the English were expecting reinforcements under the command of Sir John Falstaff. " Bastard, bastard," she said, " in God's name, I charge you, as soon as you hear of Falstaff's coming, let me know it ; for if he passes without my knowledge, I tell you, you shall lose your head." Towards evening she lay down to rest, but suddenly she started up and called d'Aulon, her squire, saying, " My *counsel* tells me to go against the English." While he was arming her, she heard voices in the street shouting that the French were suffering loss. She rushed out, and meeting her page on the way, " Ah, graceless boy !" she exclaimed, " you never told me the blood of France was being spilt." Her hostess finished arming her, then she sprang upon her horse, took her standard which the page handed her out of a window, and galloped to the eastern gate, her horse's hoofs striking sparks as she passed. At the gate she met some wounded men who were being brought in ; she stopped a moment : " I never see French blood," said she, " but the hair of my head rises up."

A small force of the besieged, eager to distinguish
D

themselves without aid from Joan or orders from
Dunois, had sallied out against the strong bastile of
St. Loup. But it was well defended by three hundred
brave Englishmen, and the assailants were suffering
for their rashness, until Joan, followed by Dunois and
a good number of troops, came to their relief. For
the first time she now saw real war, and her courage
did not fail. Standing at the edge of the fosse, she
urged her men on to the assault. The English of the
Paris bastile came and fell upon them in the rear, but
an alarm was rung from the belfry of Orleans, more
and more soldiers poured out from the city, and the
Paris men were driven back. After four or five
hours' assault, St. Loup was taken, with great
slaughter of its defenders. Among them were several
priests, whom Joan took under her protection and
sent honourably into Orleans. The French, after
plundering the bastile, set fire to it, and returned to
the city, where their victory was celebrated with
religious services and ringing of church-bells. This
first success, moderate in itself, was of immense value
to the national party, for it restored to the French
that faith in themselves of which the long series of
their defeats had almost deprived them. And their
reverse had as great an effect upon the English, who
were so used to conquering, that they had come to
regard the French as their born inferiors, meant to be
beaten and plundered. Their failure appeared to

them out of the natural course of events, a wicked miracle, a thing brought about by sorcery. The brave yeomen of Henry the Fifth were learning to fear, not any visible foe, but the unseen Enemy who had sent Joan the Witch for their destruction.

The next day, the feast of the Ascension, Joan would have had the captains follow up their success by attacking the bastile of St. Laurence, but they refused, on account of the holiness of the day. The Maid employed her enforced leisure in attending mass and exhorting her men to keep from sin and disorder. She also dictated a third and last letter to the besiegers, requiring their departure, and demanding her herald in exchange for some of the prisoners from St. Loup. She tied the letter to an arrow, and at her bidding an archer shot it into the camp, crying aloud, " Read ! Here are news !" The English having read it, shouted derisively, " News, news from the harlot of the Armagnacs !" and Joan, hearing those words, "wept abundantly, and invoked the help of God."

Meanwhile the chiefs were holding a council of war, whereat they proposed to feign an attack on some bastile north of the Loire, in order to draw the English away from their forts in the Sologne, which, thus left undefended, would be easy to take. By this means, they argued, they would hold the bridge, have free communication with the south provinces, and get

in plentiful supplies for the long siege which they
confidently expected.   Having matured this scheme,
they called Joan and told her of their intention to
attack the northern bastile, saying nothing, however,
of the real assault they had planned.   But she saw
they were hiding something from her, and bade them
speak plainly.   " I could keep greater secrets," she
said indignantly, and she walked up and down the
room with impatient steps, until Dunois quieted her
by telling her the truth.   Though she did not oppose
the scheme, it was not carried out, but a direct attack
on the south shore was arranged for the morrow.

There, as we have seen, the English held three
positions.   At the bridge-head, the bastile of the
Augustins, and the Tourelles and their boulevard,
between which was a wide and deep fosse wherein
flowed water from the Loire ; the boulevard of St.
Privé, a little below Orleans ; the bastile of St. Jean-le-
Blanc, just above the city and opposite to the islet of
St. Aignan, which only a very narrow channel
separated from the south shore.   On Friday, May
6th, Joan and about 3000 men crossed to this island,
and passed from it to the shore by an extempore
bridge of two boats.   Their landing was not opposed,
and when they reached St. Jean-le-Blanc they found
it deserted, its occupants having removed to the
bridge fortresses by order of Sir William Glasdale.
To the bridge fortresses Joan followed them, and

planted her standard before the rampart of the Augustins. But her troops had not all crossed from Orleans, and those who were with her, seeing that the English of St. Privé were coming to reinforce their fellows, were seized with fear, and hurried back to the boats. The garrison of the Augustins rushed out and pursued the fugitives with jeers and insults. The defeat of the French appeared certain, but Joan, who had been trying to cover the retreat, faced round, and with a small brave company charged the pursuers. The panic was on their side now. They saw the Witch of France riding down upon them, her charmed standard flying, her eyes flashing with terrible wrath, and they turned and fled before her into their bastiles. Once more she planted her flag before the rampart, and this time she was well supported. The bastile was taken after an obstinate defence, and to prevent riot and pillage she ordered it to be set on fire.

She would gladly have stayed with her soldiers who were left that night before the Tourelles to be ready for the next day's assault, but the chiefs, seeing that she was very weary, persuaded her to return with them into Orleans. They had another reason for parting her from the troops. While she was resting they held a council, and agreed not to renew the attack on the morrow, but recall the troops into the city, which was now well victualled, and there await reinforcements. A knight was sent to tell her

of their over-cautious decision : "God had already
done much to help them; now they would wait."
Wait!—how Joan must have hated that word! "You
have been in your council," she said, "and I have
been in mine. Be sure that God's counsel will
hold good and come to pass, and that all other
counsel shall perish." Then she turned to·Pasquerel,
who was standing near. "Rise early to-morrow,"
she said, "and keep near me all day, for I shall
have much to do, and blood shall flow above my
breast."

She rose at dawn, and after hearing mass, started
for the assault. Her host urged her to take food
before going; a shad was being got ready, he told
her. "Keep it till evening," she said gaily, "and I
will bring you a *Goddam* to eat his share." "I will
come back over the bridge," she promised.

She rode through the city, the crowd of combatants
gathering behind her; but when she reached the
Burgundy gate, she found it guarded by the governor,
Gaucourt, who had orders not to let her pass. "You
are a bad man," she said to him; "but whether you
will or no, the men-at-arms shall go out, and conquer
as they have already conquered." The people
clamoured to pass, and in their anger threatened to
kill the governor. He was forced to give way, and
Joan and the crowd rushed out to join the soldiers on
the opposite bank. Seeing she was gone, the captains

followed, and soon she was supported by Dunois and Retz, by La Hire, glad of the excuse to fight, even by the unfriendly Gaucourt himself. Every man they took with them was needed, for if the French fought for the deliverance of Orleans and the kingdom, the English were defending their ancient glory and their own lives : the fort once taken, there would be small chance of escape for any of its garrison. Under cannon-fire and through flights of arrows, the assailants leaped into the fosse and swarmed up the escarpment, "as if they believed themselves immortal." The English met them at the top ; again and again they were driven back, again and again the Maid cheered them on, crying " Fear not !—the place is yours !" At last, as if to force victory, she sprang into the fosse, and was setting a scaling-ladder against the wall when an arrow pierced her between the neck and shoulder. She was carried to a place of shelter, weeping for pain and fright ; but her strong courage soon re-asserted itself ; she drew out the arrow with her own hand, and had the wound dressed with oil, forbidding the men-at-arms to "charm" it, as they in their superstitious kindness wanted to do. She then confessed herself, and so, having cared for soul and body, hastened back to the rampart.

There was no success yet for the French, and the captains came to Joan, telling her they intended to retire and suspend the attack until next day. She besought them to persevere. She tried to break their resolve with brave words. She went to Dunois with prayers and promises. " In God's name, you shall enter shortly. Doubt not, and the English shall have no more power over you !" Her entreaties prevailed. Then she ordered the men to rest a while, eat and drink, and when they had done so, bade them renew the attack " in God's name."

She mounted her horse again and rode to a vineyard a little way off, where, out of the turmoil of battle, she prayed a few minutes. On her return she stationed herself near the rampart, holding her standard. " Watch until my banner touches the fort," she said to a gentleman who stood near. Presently the wind caught it and blew it against the wall. " It touches, Joan, it touches !" exclaimed the gentleman ; whereupon she cried to the troops, " Go in now ; all is yours !"

Meanwhile those left in Orleans had not been idle. Some of them, with planks and old wooden gutters, all pieced and joined, had contrived a bridge over that breach which Salisbury had made between the Tourelles and the Belle Croix boulevard ; others had filled a barge with slow combustibles, and, after setting them alight, had moored it under the bridge that connected the Tourelles with their boulevard. Now the men from the Belle Croix came against the English, led over their narrow and perilous bridge by a brave

knight of Rhodes, Nicole de Giresme, while the assailants of the boulevard, revived by the food they had
taken, and cheered by the Maid's presence, rushed
upon and scaled the rampart they had attacked vainly
through so many hours. The English retired towards
the Tourelles, fighting as they went, Sir William
Glasdale covering the retreat. But the fire-boat had
done its work. The half-burnt bridge gave way as
the men in armour crowded over it, and they fell,
Glasdale himself with them, into the deep water, the
weight of their armour sinking them, so that there
was no hope of rescue. Joan wept at the sight,
" having great pity on their souls," and the captains
also grieved at it, for a different reason. There were
many knights drowned from whom, had they been
taken alive, their captors would have got rich
ransoms.

By evening the Tourelles were taken, and the Loire
bridge having been hastily repaired, Joan passed over
it in triumph, and re-entered Orleans, where she and
her men were received with great joy, all the bells of
the city ringing out the news of victory. The Maid's
wound was dressed carefully, and after her usual
supper of bread with a little wine and water, she lay
down to sleep.

Very early next morning, those watching in Orleans
saw the English quit their bastiles and set themselves
before the walls in order of battle. The alarm was

given, and the French, led by Joan, came out of the
city and ranged themselves in front of their enemies.
While the armies stood face to face, as it were waiting
for a signal to begin the fight, Joan had a camp-altar
brought, and the priests said mass. Then she asked,
" Are the faces of the English towards us, or their
backs ?" She was told that they were retreating, and
at that moment flame shot up from some of their forts
which they had set on fire. " In God's name," said
Joan, " let them go. My Lord does not choose that
we shall fight to-day. You shall have them another
time."

Some of the French, led by La Hire, who could
not bear to see so much good booty march off quietly,
pursued the retreating foes, and skirmished with the
hindmost of them. Crowds rushed out from Orleans
to destroy the unburnt bastiles, and dragged back the
stores and cannon the English had been obliged to
leave. But soon the excitement of victory gave way
to the enthusiasm of thankfulness. A few days ago
the city had been surrounded by enemies, threatened
with the sword, more than threatened by famine.
But in one marvellous week God and the Maid had
delivered it. Now let her who had led the people to
victory lead them also to give thanks. They thronged
after her into the cathedral, where high mass was
celebrated. They followed her from church to church,
praising God and the saints, God and the Maid,

before their rescued altars. Night fell on their rejoicings, and early next morning the Maid left them, eager to rejoin the King, and render an account of her success. Her time for rest was not yet. She had as yet only given the *sign* promised to the doctors of Poitiers—only begun the great work she was sent to do.

CHAPTER IV.

A CAMPAIGN AND A CORONATION.

IF Joan had left her village in order to gain applause and honour, she might now have been content to rest a while and enjoy the rewards which nearly all classes were willing to give her. She had shown her sign, and there were few who did not accept it ; but those few, unfortunately, were just the men who were closest to the King, and had most influence over him.

Scholars, high in place, great in learning, paid her their tribute of praise. The famous Gerson wrote from his monastery at Lyons, comparing her to heroes of the Old Testament and saints of the New, exhorting the heads of the nation to trust in her, warning them, almost prophetically, not to let "unbelief, ingratitude, or other injustice" render useless the divine help given through her. Jacques Gelu, the Archbishop of Embrun, wrote in the same strain, and even more plainly and warmly. But the common people were her most eager admirers and lovers. During her journey from Orleans to Tours, they crowded about her, trying to touch her hands, her dress, the trappings of her horse—even stooping down to kiss the hoof-prints of her horse on the road.

Charles came to meet her at Tours. When she knelt before him, he took off his cap, as to a queen, raised her, and seemed "as if he gladly would have kissed her, for the joy he had." He would have ennobled her at once, and he desired her to take for her arms the lilies of France, with a royal crown and a sword drawn to defend it. Empty honours and easy lip-gratitude were at her service, but she, who had one only noble ambition, cared nothing for them. She wanted but one boon from the King—ready action. Now was the time to go to Reims, while the English were weakened and disheartened, before they could forget their defeat, bring reinforcements, have their child-King anointed with the sacred oil. Let the King come—she would conduct him there safely and without hindrance—but let him come at once, for she had much to do, and little time wherein to do it. "Make use of me," she pleaded, "for I shall last only one year."

Her bold proposal amazed Charles and his council. Go to Reims, to a city held by the English, through a country guarded by hostile troops! Imperil the King's person, to say nothing of the persons of La

Tremouille and the other ease-lovers of the court! Excuses were plentiful. The King had no money to pay an army. The English were powerful still, and close at hand in their fortresses on the Loire. He who was not England's servant in the north was the servant of Burgundy. Charles listened placidly to his advisers, and came to no decision.

But one day Joan went to him at his castle of Loches, and found him in close consultation with three of his most honest councillors, Robert de Maçon, a former chancellor of France, Christopher d'Harcourt, and his confessor. She threw herself at his feet and embraced his knees. "Gracious Dauphin," she said, "hold not so many nor such long councils, but come quickly to Reims and receive your crown."

Christopher d'Harcourt asked her if her voices had bidden her speak thus. She answered, Yes; and he further wished to know in what manner the voices addressed her. She blushed greatly, and the King, touched by her emotion, inquired whether she was willing to speak before those gentlemen. She was very willing, she said, and she told how, whenever men's doubts and opposition grieved her, she went apart and prayed, complaining to God of their unbelief, until at last a *voice* came to her, which said, "Daughter of God, go on, go on; I will be thy help!" Her face glowed with joy as she repeated those words. She rejoiced greatly, she said, when-ever she heard them, and would gladly be always in that state.

The King, half-persuaded, agreed to go to Reims, but not until the English had been driven from the Loire. The captains declared that it would be unwise to march northward while the southern provinces remained so exposed to the enemy, and Joan, whose good sense equalled her courage, deferred to their judgment. An army was assembled, and put under command of the Duke of Alençon, who had now paid the last instalment of his ransom; but the King required him to do nothing without the Maid's advice. While she was near Charles, and her brave words were in his ears, he almost believed in her.

Joan went to Selles to prepare for the campaign. Among those who came to join the army were two kinsmen of La Tremouille, Guy and André de Laval, whose widowed mother was anxious that they should be placed near the King's person. But the young men saw Joan, listened to her, and went wild with youthful enthusiasm for her. Guy wrote about her to his mother and grandmother. The King, he told them, had received him graciously, and presented him to the Maid, who had ridden out from Selles to meet the royal party. " When we alighted at Selles, I went to see her at her lodging, and she had wine brought, and told me she would soon make me drink wine in Paris ; and to see her and hear her, she seems altogether divine." That same day, June 6th, she left Selles with part of the army, and the young lord watched her set out. " I saw her mount," he wrote, "all in white armour except her head, on a great black charger, which curveted greatly in front of her lodging, and would not let her mount. Then she said, ' Take him to the cross,' which was before the church. And she mounted, he moving no more than if he had been tied. Then she turned towards the church door, which was close by, and said in a pleasant woman's voice, ' You priests and churchmen, make a procession and prayers to God.' She then rode on, saying, ' Forward, forward!' — her furled banner being carried by a comely page, and her little axe in her hand." He was eager to accompany Joan, but she, knowing his mother's desire, begged him to wait and attend the King to Reims. " But," he wrote in his eagerness, " God can never choose me to do so, and not to go, and my brother says the same, as does also my Lord of Alençon."

On the 9th of June, just a month after her departure from Orleans, Joan returned there with her army. During the campaign she made the city her head-quarters, to the delight of its people, who " could not have enough of gazing at her." On the 11th, she led the troops against Jargeau, a strong town, held by

Suffolk and about seven hundred picked men. The French had heard that Falstaff was on his way to reinforce the garrison, and many of them, who had not overcome their old fear of the English, wished to draw back. Some, indeed, did retire, but Joan's words of faith kept most of them faithful. She said, "If I were not sure that God is guiding this work, I would rather keep sheep than expose myself to so many dangers." That evening the suburbs were taken, and Joan summoned the garrison to surrender, offering to let them depart in safety, but without their armour. Suffolk demanded a fortnight's truce, which was refused, and next morning Joan gave orders for the assault. The Duke of Alençon would have put it off, but she bade him not doubt, for that was God's time. "Ah, noble Duke," she said, "are you afraid? Know you not that I promised your wife to bring you back safe and sound?" Before her first departure for Orleans, she had passed some days with the Duchess, who was a daughter of the captive Duke Charles.

Jargeau was bravely defended, but the assailants had the advantage of numbers, and, once their fears were forgotten, went boldly to the attack. Joan and the Duke, commanders though they were, went down into the fosse like the rest, and the Maid was climbing a scaling-ladder, when a stone hurled from the rampart struck her to the earth. But she was up in a moment,

E

shouting, " Friends, friends, go on ! Our Lord has condemned the English ! They are ours ! Be of good courage !" The men swarmed over the walls, and the place was taken. Suffolk was hard pressed by a young squire who summoned him to yield. "Are you a gentleman ?" inquired the earl. "Yes." "Are you a knight ?" "No." The earl would surrender only to his equal, so he first knighted the squire, and then gave him his sword. About five hundred of the garrison fell during the attack, and many who had been made prisoners were killed afterwards by the soldiers, who were very loath to give quarter. The more important captives were sent down the Loire to Orleans, where Joan and Alençon returned the day after their victory.

On June 15th the French took the fortified bridge of Meun, and early next day advanced upon Baugency, which place, like Jargeau, was garrisoned chiefly by the late besiegers of Orleans. On the approach of Joan's army, most of the English retired into the castle, leaving the town undefended, except by a few brave men who were resolved the enemy should not have it without a struggle. These were soon overcome, and the French prepared to storm the castle. In the midst of their preparations, news came to them that Arthur of Richmond was approaching with a large force. Alençon was much perplexed. The King had ordered him to have nothing to do with the disgraced Constable, but Joan and the captains were anxious to receive him. The Duke at first threatened to resign his command if Richmond were accepted, but Joan overcame his scruples. She promised to make the Constable's peace with Charles, and he and his Bretons were allowed to join the army.

Meanwhile, Falstaff and Talbot had met and united their forces. On the 17th they entered Meun, and spent the night in cannonading the bridge, intending to cross by it and go to the relief of Baugency. But early next day they heard that Baugency had capitulated, and they marched northward, taking the garrison of Meun with them. The French followed, but the Beauce country was wild, depopulated by war, overgrown with thickets, and the leaders, uncertain which way the enemy had gone, doubted the wisdom of advancing. But Joan bade them ride on, promising them "sure guidance." Near Patay they came upon the English, who had been warned of their approach, and were getting ready for battle. The vanguard and artillery had taken up their position on the edge of a little wood, the approach to which was protected by Talbot with a chosen body of archers, while Falstaff and the centre of the army waited to join him until the rear-guard should have come up.

The Duke of Alençon asked Joan what was to

be done. "Have you good spurs?" she inquired.
"What!" exclaimed some who stood by; "should
we turn our backs?" "Not so, in God's name!" she
answered. "The English shall do that. They will
be beaten, and you will want your spurs to pursue
them."

Some of the chiefs hung back. They had taken
strong towns from the English, but since Joan's
coming they had not met them in the open field, and
traditions of Crécy and Poitiers and memories of
Agincourt and Verneuil were present with them.
Joan saw their hesitation. "In God's name, we must
fight them!" she cried. "Though they were hung to
the clouds, we should have them. To-day the King
shall have the greatest victory he has won for long.
My *counsel* tells me they are ours." She wished to
advance at once, but she was kept back, and La Hire
was sent to begin the attack. He rushed impetuously
on the English rear, and put it to flight, but Talbot
held his place, and Falstaff tried to join him, according to the plan they had agreed on. The vanguard,
however, seeing the main body of the army moving
away from the French, imagined it was retreating,
and fled. Falstaff would now have turned upon the
French, but it was too late, for the victory was theirs.
The English artillery was surrounded; brave Talbot
was taken prisoner; the battle was no longer a battle,
but a rout. Falstaff, by the advice of his captains,

fled with a small company, and for that failure in courage he was deprived for some time of his order of the Garter. In slain and prisoners the English had lost nearly 3000 men. Joan was very indignant at the cruelty of the victors. Seeing one of them strike down a wounded prisoner, she sprang from her horse, raised the poor soldier in her arms, and held him thus while he confessed to a priest whom she had sent for, tenderly comforting him until he died. It was always so with her. Before and during the fight, she was the stern champion of France; but when it was over, she became again a pitying woman, weeping for her dead enemies, and praying for their souls.

La Hire's charge had won the battle of Patay, and the battle of Patay ended the campaign of the Loire. The whole district turned against the English. Janville closed its gates against Falstaff, and he retreated towards Paris, leaving nearly all Beauce to the conquerors.

Now Joan held her rightful place in the army. Every true and honest man believed in her; even those who had doubted her at Orleans confessed now not only her goodness and courage, but also the instinctive military skill she had shown both in sieges and in the field. Soldiers and leaders were alike eager to follow her to Reims. With nothing to consult and combat but their frank likes and dislikes, her task would have been an easy one; but to do her voices' bidding, she had to hew or wind her way through the intrigues of a court, and of as vile a creature as ever a court had nourished.

On Sunday, June 19th, Joan returned to Orleans, where she hoped to find the King. The inhabitants earnestly desired his presence, and were making glad preparations to receive him ; but he was La Tremouille's guest at Sully-sur-Loire, and the favourite artfully dissuaded him from visiting the city Joan had rescued. Had Charles ridden through its gaily-decked streets, heard the people's shouts, held unchecked converse with the Maid and her good knights, he must have caught some enthusiasm from the place and hour—have felt some stirring of royal pride and patriotic zeal. And any wholesome emotion would have weakened La Tremouille's influence, and inclined the King to shake off those debasing bonds which kept him from all kingliness of thought and deed.

Joan, with Alençon and some other nobles, went to Sully to plead Richmond's cause. After a good deal of persuasion, Charles pardoned the man who had brought fifteen hundred men to fight for him, but neither the Maid nor the captains could induce him to let the Constable go with the army to Reims ; La Tremouille's influence was stronger than any of theirs. Indeed, Charles demurred at going to Reims at all. He hated trouble, and his life in the south had on the whole been pleasant enough. All Joan's victories had as yet done him no substantial good. He was as poor as ever, and the excited men who flocked to the Maid's banner were to him objects less of pride than of distrust.

The Maid, foreseeing more delays, sick at heart of his apathy, could not control her tears, and he, bewildered by a grief he could not understand, spoke to her kindly, paid her many compliments, and advised her to take some rest. Still weeping, she besought him to have faith, promising that he should recover his kingdom and be crowned before long. At last the troops were ordered to assemble at Gien, and Joan went to Orleans to make preparations. On Friday, June 24th, she brought the army of the Loire to Gien, whence she sent a letter to the loyal city of Tournay, telling its people of her late successes, and praying them to come to the coronation.

But the coronation seemed as far off as ever. Charles held frequent councils, where all sorts of plans were discussed. The captains who lately had been so eager to obey Joan were cooling a little towards her in that cold atmosphere. Some of them proposed an expedition against Rouen; some advised the conquest of La Charité and other Loire fortresses still held by the enemy; others again approved of the journey to Reims, but wished to defer it until the

Queen could safely accompany her husband. Joan
was against them all. Let them do what they would
afterwards—fight the English on the Seine or on the
Loire; but first let France have her rights—let Charles
the Dauphin go and be made King! Two days after
her arrival at Gien, the justly-impatient girl quitted
the town with some of her troops and encamped in
the fields beyond it. Her persistence carried the day.
On the 29th, the King and an army of 12,000 men set
out for Reims.

On July 1st they arrived before Auxerre in Burgundy. The inhabitants would not admit the King,
but promised to surrender if Troyes, Châlons, and
Reims did so. It was said that they paid La Tremouille a bribe of two thousand crowns for leave to
remain neutral. Joan would have forced them to
submit, but her advice was not taken, and the army
went on to St. Florentin, which yielded at the first
summons. On the 5th it reached Troyes, the city
where France had been signed away from its rightful
heir. Joan had written to the citizens, requiring them
to receive the King, and Charles also bade them
surrender, promising them amnesty and easy terms.
But the place was well garrisoned, and they determined to resist. They wrote to Reims and other
cities, demanding reinforcements, and telling how
they had burnt the letter of the Maid, whom they
called a witch and instrument of Satan. The garrison

made a sortie, which was repulsed, and the royal army encamped before the walls.

There was within the city a famous enthusiast called Friar Richard, who had been going about France preaching and uttering vague prophecies, which were afterwards applied to the Maid's coming and the King's successes. " Sow, good people, sow !" he had cried ; " sow beans in plenty, for he that shall come will come shortly." Now he desired to see the Maid, whom, however, he half-feared, thinking she might be all her enemies called her ; so he came out to her, crossing himself and sprinkling holy water. "Approach boldly," she called to him ; " I shall not fly away !" Having convinced him that she was no messenger of the devil, she sent him back into Troyes with another letter, which was as useless as the first.

Five days had now been spent before Troyes, and famine began to be felt in the camp. The soldiers had hardly any food except the beans which had been sown abundantly in obedience to Friar Richard's command. A council was held, and nearly all who were at it advised raising the siege and returning southward, Regnault de Chartres and La Tremouille being most in favour of that cowardly movement. But among those faint hearts was one man who believed in Joan—Robert le Maçon, the old chancellor who had heard her appeal to Charles at

Loches—and he spoke boldly for her. "When the King undertook this journey, he did it not because of the great might of the men-at-arms, nor because of the great wealth he had, nor because the journey seemed possible to him, but because Joan told him to go forward and be crowned at Reims, such being the good pleasure of God." While he was yet speaking, Joan herself knocked at the door; she was let in, and the Archbishop told her the cause of the debate.

She turned to the King. "Will you believe me?" she asked. "Speak," he replied, "and if you speak reasonably and profitably, we will gladly believe you."

"Will you believe me?" she said again. "Yes," repeated Charles, "according to what you say." That cold answer might well have checked her, but she spoke on: "Gracious King of France, if you will remain before your city of Troyes, it shall be yours within three days by force or by love—doubt it not." "We would wait six, if we could be sure of having it," said the Archbishop. "Doubt not," she insisted, "you shall have it to-morrow."

It was then evening, but she at once mounted her horse and began preparations for an assault. Her energy cheered the soldiers, who were weary of their five days' inaction. They dragged the cannons into position, and brought bundles of wood, doors, furniture, everything they could lay hands on, to fill up the fosse. They worked far into the night — leaders, pages, men-at-arms alike — Joan directing them "better than two of the best captains could have done."

Through that night there was great excitement within Troyes. The people had heard of Orleans and Jargeau; they could see and hear Joan's preparations; Friar Richard went among them, exhorting them to return to their lawful sovereign. At last they asked loudly why they, French by birth, should risk their city and their lives for England or Burgundy. A council was held, and the heads of the garrison and of the city agreed to surrender. Early next morning, just as Joan was giving the signal for the assault, the city gates were opened, and the bishop, with a deputation of burgesses and captains, came out and asked to see the King. Charles received them graciously, confirmed the promises he had already given, and engaged to let the garrison depart with all their goods. The next day, Sunday, he entered the town in state, attended by Joan and his nobles. The English and Burgundians were going out as had been agreed, but among them Joan saw some woful French prisoners, and she sprang forward, saying these should not quit the place. The soldiers argued that their property had been secured to them, and that prisoners of war *were* property; but she said, "In God's name, they shall not go!" and kept them with her. The King paid a small ransom for them to their disappointed captors.

Next day the King and army left Troyes. They approached Châlons. on the 15th, and at some distance from the town were met by a number of citizens who had come to offer their submission. At Châlons, Joan had the great joy of meeting some friends' from Domremy. She asked them many questions about her home, and they looked with wonder at the girl who lived familiarly with princes, and yet spoke and behaved as simply as ever she had done in the days of her obscurity. One of them inquired whether she feared nothing. " Nothing but treachery," was her foreboding answer.

While Joan had been winning victories for the Dauphin, and leading him towards his crown, Bedford had been striving and intriguing in the cause of his nephew. *She* had succeeded by arousing men's nobler feelings—their loyalty, their patriotism, and devotion ; *he* had only their baser passions to work upon—their self-interest, ambition, and desire for vengeance. Each day showed him more plainly that in France, even in those parts where the English had ruled well, the people had no love for them, and that the country could be kept only by the strong hand. He pretended to believe that Joan's victories were brought about by the power of evil. The doctrine held comfort for the nation that had seen its best generals and finest soldiers beaten by a young peasant-woman. After the discomfiture before Orleans, he wrote to the English King and Parliament, announcing and accounting for the disaster. " There felle by the hand of God, as it seemeth, a great strook upon your peuple that was assembled there in grete nombre, caused in grete partie, as y trowe, of lakke of sadde beleve, and of unlevefulle doubte that thei hadde of a disciple and lyme of the Feende called the Pucelle, that used fals enchauntments and sorcerie." He had found difficulty in raising the army that was lost at Patay, and now the Parliament, weary of the long war, showed no readiness to supply another in its place. So he looked for aid to his uncle, Henry Beaufort, the rich and restless cardinal-bishop of Winchester, and to Burgundy. The cardinal had just collected an army for a crusade against the Hussites, and Bedford prevailed on him to let it serve first in the French war. How could soldiers of the Church, he argued, be better employed than in fighting against Hell itself in the person of Joan, that "lyme of the Feende"? He persuaded the Duke of Burgundy to visit Paris, where he received him with great honour, and reminded him in every possible way of his father's unavenged murder. The plan answered well. Philip and all the friends of Burgundy swore anew their undying enmity to Charles and the Armagnacs.

From the day when Charles left Gien, the Anglo-Burgundians had plied Reims with letters and messages, exhorting it to hold out until Winchester's army should come to its rescue, warning it not to imitate those towns that had opened their gates to the Dauphin, ridiculing the Maid, and belittling her exploits. Letters came to Reims from all quarters—from Charles, calling upon it to receive him; from Troyes and Châlons, first charging it to follow their example and resist, then advising it to follow their example and yield. For a while, the citizens played a double part, promising fidelity to England even while declining to receive an English or Burgundian garrison. But when they had the second letter from Troyes, and one from their own Archbishop expressing the King's good-will towards them; when they heard that Châlons had submitted, and that Charles was within four leagues of them, they sent deputies to tender their obedience, and that same day, Saturday, July 16th, Charles entered the city.

Preparations were at once made for his coronation, and early next morning four nobles went to the abbey of St. Remi to escort thence the ampulla containing the sacred oil which a dove had brought from heaven to the saint. The abbot, in full canonicals, carried it to the cathedral, where the Archbishop of Reims received it from him, and set it on the high altar. Below the altar stood the Dauphin, attended by the

nobles and clergy who acted as proxies for the peers
of France who should have been with him. By his
side was Joan, holding her sacred banner. The
ceremony was performed according to the ancient
rites, and when it was over, Joan knelt at the feet of
Charles, her King indeed now, crowned and anointed.
"Gracious King," she said, "now is fulfilled the
pleasure of God, whose will it was that you should
come to Reims to receive your worthy coronation,
showing that you are the true King to whom the
kingdom should belong." As she spoke she wept,
and all who were in the church wept for sympathy.
Among those who witnessed her triumph was her
father, who had come to Reims to see her. The good
peasant was honourably treated ; the corporation of
the town paid his expenses, and when he returned to
Domremy, gave him a horse for the journey.

In June the Maid had written to Philip of Burgundy, begging him to come to the coronation. On
the morning of the ceremony she wrote to him again.
"I charge you," she said, "by the King of Heaven,
my true and sovereign Lord, that you and the King
of France make a good and sure peace that shall last
long. Forgive one another, from your hearts, entirely,
as becomes loyal Christians. . . . And I pray
and entreat you with clasped hands to make war
with us no more ; and be sure that whatever number
of men you bring against us, they shall gain nothing,

and there shall be much sorrow because of the great battle and the slaughter of those that come against us." The letter was probably carried to Philip by some delegates whom he had secretly sent ·to the King. His lately-sworn friendship to England, and newly-revived anxiety to avenge his father's death, were not strong enough to keep him from attending to his own interests. He returned no answer to Joan, and apparently was nowise moved by her simple entreaties.

CHAPTER V.

FAILURES.

AFTER his coronation, when Charles was bestowing honours and rewards on his followers, Joan asked him for one favour, which he granted readily—freedom from taxation for her native Domremy and the adjoining village of Greux. For herself she wanted nothing, except what she had already claimed and failed to receive, what the King never gave her—his trust.

She had given a King to France, now she had to give France to her King. And beyond the expulsion of the English, she had set herself another task, the deliverance of Charles of Orleans from captivity. She longed to be again at work. Every day of waiting was a day of pain to her. Now that her King was crowned, she would have him press forward to Paris, defy the English, and startle the disloyal French into loyalty; but the evil advice of his courtiers and his own indolence made him catch at every excuse for delay. His loitering gave Bedford

F

time to strengthen his party, and bring to the capital Winchester's five thousand men, whom he had gone to meet on their landing.

On July 21st, Charles went to the Abbey of St. Marcoul, near Reims, to touch for "the evil," as was customary for all newly-crowned Kings of France. Next day he went to Vailly, where the keys of Soissons and Laon were brought to him, and on the morrow, at Soissons, he received the submission of four other towns. His journey was a triumphal progress. But the courtiers, who had always shown an evil ingenuity in baffling Joan, contrived, by means of this very success which was owing to her, to thwart her plans. It was pleasant and dignified work to go from town to town, receiving keys from obedient burgesses ; and as places south of the road to Paris sent in offers of submission, what more natural than to turn aside a little towards the Loire? And the Loire once approached, what more prudent than to go on, cross it, and get back into Berry, leaving Paris to be won by negotiations with the Duke of Burgundy, without any more fuss or fighting, or glory for the Maid?

On August 4th, the King arrived at Bray, on the left bank of the Seine. The inhabitants had agreed to let the army cross the river, and it encamped for the night on the right bank. But, during the night, a party of English entered the town, and next morning, when the French attempted to cross, they were repulsed.

A passage might have been forced, but the troops were being taken southward against their will, and would have put little heart into their fighting. There was no choice but to march back towards Paris. However, the Archbishop and La Trémouille, foiled on one point, were successful on another—they persuaded Charles to sign a truce with the Duke of Burgundy.

Joan at once sent news of it to the people of Reims, who were disquieted at the change in the King's plans :—

" My dear and good friends, the loyal French of the city of Reims, Joan the Maid sends you tidings of herself, and prays you not to doubt the good quarrel she carries on for the blood-royal. I promise and certify I will never forsake you while I live. It is true that the King has made a truce for fifteen days with the Duke of Burgundy, by which he is to surrender Paris peacefully at the end of that time. Yet do not marvel if I enter it not so soon, for I am not content with truces made thus, and I know not if I shall keep them; but if I do keep them, it will be only to guard the King's honour. They shall not make light of the blood-royal, for I will keep and hold together the King's army, and be ready at the end of these fifteen days if they do not make peace. Therefore, my very dear and perfect friends, I pray you not to disquiet yourselves, but to keep good watch, and guard the King's city. Let me know if there be any traitors who would harm you, and as soon as I can I will take them away. And let me have news of you. God, to whom I commend you, have you in His keeping.

" Written on Friday, the fifth day of August, in camp, on the road to Paris."

This letter, which might have been written by a proud and grieved queen, seems to mark a change in the Maid ; a change wrought, not by any devotion or homage that had been paid to her—for love never harmed one like her—but by the hardening and embittering treatment she had received from the King and the Court. Every plan of hers had been suspected, carped at, thwarted as much as possible, and yet every plan had succeeded through her own courage and constancy. No wonder she was self-assured, and spoke of acting without advice or orders. " I am not content with truces made thus ; I know not if I shall keep them." The haughty words were doubtless reported to Charles, and turned to her injury.

During the northward march of the army, people from every place on the road crowded to welcome Joan and the King, crying Noël, Noël, and singing *Te Deums* before them. Joan was first. They were glad to have a French King again, but their chief love and enthusiasm were for her, the heroic girl in shining armour, with her calm face and gentle voice. The common folk called her " the angelic ;" they sang songs about her ; images of her were put up in little country churches ; a special collect was said at mass, thanking God for having saved France by a woman ; medals were struck in her honour, and worn as amulets. The people pressed about her horse, and kissed her hands and feet. She was often vexed by this excess of homage, which brought upon her the displeasure of many churchmen.

Near Crespy, as she, riding between Dunois and Regnault de Chartres, passed through the welcoming crowd, she said, " What good people! I have yet seen none so joyful at the coming of their prince. May I be so happy as to die and be buried in this land!" " Oh, Joan," said the Archbishop, " in what place do you expect to die?" " Wherever it shall please God," she answered, " for I know not the place nor the hour any more than yourself. Would to God that I might return now, and lay down my arms, and go back to serve my parents, and guard their flocks with my sister and brothers, who would be right glad to see me." She must often have longed for her home, but never except this once did she express her longing. She had a rare reticence for one so young and simple. " She spoke little, and showed a marvellous prudence in her words."

At Crespy, Charles received from Bedford a contemptuous and insulting letter, taxing him with having wrongfully claimed the crown from Henry, "the true and natural lord of France and England," and with "deceiving the people by aid of a disorderly and infamous woman." The Regent further declared that he had taken the field in person, and invited

Charles to meet him at some appointed place and time, either to decide their quarrel by the sword, or to arrange a peace, " not false, corrupt, violated, and perjured, like that of Montereau."

Even Charles was stung by this letter, and the army had orders to advance. The vanguard reached Dammartin on the 13th, and found Bedford a little distance off, but so advantageously posted that it would have been folly to attack him. That night the English returned to Paris for reinforcements, and on the following day took up a very strong position near Senlis. The French, who had heard of this movement too late to interrupt it, found them, on the 15th, drawn up in battle array, with the banners of France and England floating over them.

Yet there was no battle. There were sharp skirmishes, in one of which La Trémouille came near being killed ; but Bedford kept the main part of his army in its safe position, though Joan rode up to his very entrenchments and challenged him to fight in the open. He probably hoped to wear out the patience of the French, and provoke them to an onset as wild and daring as those which had lost Crécy and Poitiers to their ancestors.

In the evening Charles returned to Crespy ; but he left Joan and the army on the field, and next morning they feigned a retreat, hoping that Bedford might be tempted to pursue them. But about noon they heard that he was marching towards Paris, and as he had gone too far for them to follow, they rejoined the King.

From Crespy, Charles summoned various towns in the neighbourhood to surrender. Compiègne was the first to obey, and the King went there on the 18th. Senlis and Beauvais soon followed its example. When the royal herald arrived at Beauvais, he was greeted with a tumult of joy, the people singing *Te Deums*, and shouting, " Long live Charles, King of France," to the great anger of their bishop, Pierre Cauchon, an avowed friend of England and Burgundy. He and all the other disloyal French in the city were forced to leave it, and he carried with him feelings of bitterness and hatred which, later on, bore terrible fruit.

The truce was now over, and it became clear that Philip either could not or would not procure the surrender of Paris. But neither did he choose just then to quarrel openly with Charles, and so he sent John of Luxembourg to Compiègne, to speak him fair, and so flatter him with hopes of a general peace as to obtain a renewal of the truce. The King's blind and foolish advisers still favoured Burgundy, and expected to get Paris by his means. The King himself was well content to put off or escape from warfare. But Joan was eager to be stirring, to make an end of negotiations which her common sense told her were worse than useless. At last, without leave or counsel, she said to Alençon, " Fair Duke, have ready your men and those of the other captains, for I must go and see Paris nearer than I have seen it yet." Alençon, who was almost as impatient as herself, obeyed her gladly; on the 23rd the army left Compiègne, and in three days it arrived at St. Denis.

Just as Joan was setting out, a letter was brought to her from the Count of Armagnac, then in Aragon, inquiring of her, as of an oracle, which of the three contenders for the Papacy was the true Pope of God's choosing. She answered that, being busy with the war, she could then give no sure reply, but promised to send one from Paris. That same month the schism in the Church came to an end, and the tiara was assured to Martin V.

Joan greatly desired the King's arrival before Paris, believing that his mere presence would make its gates fly open like those of Reims and Soissons. In that she was mistaken. The Burgundians were very strong within the city, and however Philip might temporise, his party hated Charles as an Armagnac and a personal enemy. The populace might have been glad to receive him, but their ignorance and fears had been artfully worked upon. The King, they were told, had sworn to abandon Paris, and every man, woman, and child in it, to his ferocious soldiery, and to drive the plough over the place where the city had been ; while

Joan, " the Witch of the Armagnacs," was represented to them as a creature horrible and wicked beyond the power of words to describe. Bedford was confident that the capital could be taken only by force ; and as he feared for Normandy, where La Hire and Arthur of Richmond had been very successful, he went there with a large body of English, leaving Paris in charge of able lieutenants.

The King lingered at Senlis, disregarding the urgent messages that were sent to him. By Joan's desire, Alençon went twice to fetch him, and the second time succeeded in bringing him to St. Denis, where the troops hailed his coming as an earnest of victory. " Now," they said, " the Maid will put him inside Paris, if it depends only on her."

The King's folly and the ill-will of his favourites were not Joan's only troubles. The army before Paris was not like that chosen army she had led to Orleans, a company of men " confessed, penitent," who for the time seemed purified from evil desires, and followed her as to a holy war. Such a state of things, fair to the eye, but born only of the froth and ecstasy of religion, could not last, as the Maid in her young confidence perhaps expected. She had now to grieve because of her soldiers' habits of blasphemy and pillage, and the shameless women who came about the camp. These were usually kept out of her sight, but at St. Denis one of them came flaunting before

her, and the indignant Maid struck her with the flat
of her sword.   It was the sword of St. Catherine, and
the sacred blade broke, as if indignant at being put to
such unworthy use.   Joan, who was not superstitious,
girded on another weapon which she had taken in
battle, but the people saw in the mishap an omen of
evil.   Even the King was vexed by it, and told her
she should have taken a good stick for such
work.

On September 6th, the day before the King's
arrival, most of the troops had moved to La Chapelle,
a village between St. Denis and Paris.   On the
morning of the 8th, the festival of the Virgin's
nativity, they advanced to attack the city.   They
were divided into two corps.   One, led by Joan, Gaucourt, and Retz, went at once to the assault, while the
other, under command of Alençon and Clermont,
remained in reserve a little way off.   The attack
began about noon ; the bastion of the St. Honoré
gate having been set on fire, its defenders were forced
to abandon it, and the assailants, headed by Joan,
passed the outer fosse.   She climbed the ridge
separating it from the inner fosse, which was full of
water, and from that place summoned the city to
surrender.   She was answered with jeers and insults
and a shower of missiles, amid which she carefully
sounded the fosse with her lance, and found that it
was of unusual depth.   At her bidding the men

brought faggots and hurdles to fill it up and make a resting-place for their ladders, but while she was directing them, an arrow wounded her in the thigh so severely that she was forced to lie down at the edge of the fosse. She suffered, as she afterwards confessed, agonies of pain, but she never ceased to encourage her men, bidding them advance boldly, for the place would be taken. The place would have been taken. Within, the Armagnacs and secret loyalists were crying about the streets that there was no hope, that the city must fall, and the populace, who were crowding the churches, rushed out wildly and shut themselves into their houses. Their infectious terror would have been a good ally for the King.

But the captains who were with Joan, seeing that the hours went by and the men were struck down without achieving much—perhaps really convinced that for that day further efforts were useless, determined to retire. Gaucourt was standing near the Maid, and she passionately implored him to wait—to go on with the attack—" the city *must* be taken," she said. But the jealous old soldier, who had always opposed her, was deaf now also to her pleading, and ordered a retreat. The trumpets sounded ; the men withdrew. Joan, desperate in her sorrow, clung to the ground, declaring she would not go until the place was won. At about ten o'clock Gaucourt had her removed by force and set upon her horse. She was carried back to La Chapelle, suffering in body, suffering more in mind, but still resolute. "The city would have been taken!" she insisted. "It would have been taken!"

She was resolved to take it. Her wound was dressed that night, and next day she went betimes to Alençon and prayed him to order another assault. "I will not quit the city until it is ours!" she said. The Duke did her bidding, and even while the troops were assembling, they were joined by the Lord of Montmorenci and fifty gentlemen, who had left Paris to fight on the patriotic side. Their coming was a good omen, and the army was advancing gladly, when a message came from the King, ordering it to turn back, and desiring the Maid's presence at St. Denis.

Still Joan would not give up. In spite of himself she would give Paris to the King. Alençon had made a bridge over the Seine at St. Denis, and she determined to cross by it and attack the city at a different point. She held counsel with her trusty captains, and they agreed to renew the assault on the morrow. On the morrow they set out very early, full of hope, but when they arrived at the river the bridge was gone. It had been destroyed during the night, and the King himself, who had found out their plan, had commanded the suicidal crime.

He had won a deplorable victory over his best

friends, and now he spoke openly of returning southward for reinforcements, as he said, and because
of the truce with Burgundy. Joan and Alençon
entreated him not to leave Paris untaken, nor
abandon the loyal towns of the Isle-of-France to his
enemies' vengeance; but their pleading was in vain,
and when the Maid saw that she could not prevail,
she went to the abbey-church of St. Denis and hung
up her armour there as an offering to the Virgin and
to the saint whose name was the war-cry of France.
She at first refused to leave St. Denis; her saints, she
said, had commanded her to remain; but she was
persuaded to go with the army, " against her Lord's
will."

Charles spent the last days of his stay in holding
councils and providing very inefficiently for the protection of the Isle-of-France. Clermont was made
governor of the province; Vendôme was left at St.
Denis with a small force to cover the King's retreat.
With what bitterness of heart must Joan have
watched those pitiful preparations!

The royal deserter left St. Denis on the 13th. He
who had gone so slowly, so unwillingly, to receive his
crown, went so quickly now that the march was
almost a flight. As he hurried onward, his army
dispersed. Some of the soldiers were left in garrison
towns, but many of them scattered over the country
and took up their old freebooting habits. When the

King arrived before Sens with a disorderly remnant, the inhabitants shut their gates against him, and he turned aside and crossed the Yonne by a ford near the city. On the 21st he reached Gien, and the miserable journey was over.

Before then its evil results had begun. Charles had hardly turned his back upon Paris, when the Count of Vendôme followed his example and removed to Senlis, leaving St. Denis to the mercy of the English, who came down on it and plundered at their will. Clermont, pursuing his master's policy, extended the benefit of the truce to Paris and its neighbourhood, and in a few days the Duke of Burgundy brought 6000 Picard soldiers into the capital. Bedford, who had now returned, spared no sacrifice to bind Philip to the English cause. He appointed him his lieutenant in France, gave him lordship over Champagne, and made him guardian of Paris, keeping for himself only the name of Regent and the government of Normandy. About the middle of October he returned to Normandy with his English troops, and shortly afterwards Philip went back to Flanders to prepare for his third marriage, taking his Picards with him. "Great thieves" the Parisians had found them, but when they were gone the city was left almost undefended, and brigand companies ravaged the country to its very walls. No one dared to venture beyond them, for fear of being killed or captured. Provisions could seldom be brought in, and there was great scarcity. But the sufferings of Paris were light compared to those of the province. Places that had yielded to Charles were taken and pillaged not only by the English, but by the Burgundians also, whom no truce could deter from such profitable warfare. Then they were retaken and pillaged anew by loyal troops turned brigands, for whom the hateful name of Armagnacs was now revived. The country, that had been tolerably prosperous under English rule, was ravaged far and wide till it became a desert. The peasantry fled, or perished of the hardships they had to undergo. It was a winter of horrors for the wretched people, and they had good cause to regret having welcomed their unsteadfast King.

When Charles crossed the Loire, the remainder of his army disbanded, and Alençon returned to his own territory. But he did not rest long. La Hire was fighting in Normandy, and the Duke, who had estates in that province, was eager to join him. He asked the King to let Joan go with him on the campaign, for he knew that the best soldiers in France would assemble round her standard. Joan longed to go, but the King's rulers—Gaucourt, La Trémouille, and the cautious Archbishop—were against her, and the King refused his consent. Alençon left the Court, and she and her "fair Duke" never met again.

But another expedition was arranged for her.

Early in November she was sent with the Sire d'Albert, La Trémouille's half-brother, to drive the English from their position on the upper Loire. The troops met at Bourges, and went first to besiege St. Pierre-le-Moustier, a small but well-fortified place. Their first attack was repulsed, and they fled in disorder; but Joan, as if unconcious of their flight, stayed close to the fosse with only four or five brave men. D'Aulon, who was disabled by a wound in the foot, mounted a horse and hastened to bring her out of her peril. He asked her why she was there alone, and she, raising her helmet, looked at him as if not understanding his words. She was not alone, she told him; fifty thousand of her men were with her, and she would not move until the town was taken. " Go," she cried—" go, all of you ; bring faggots and hurdles to make a bridge!" The amazed soldiers heard her ; they thought she had the hosts of heaven with her, and they came back to the walls. The assault was fiercely renewed, the place was taken, and Joan used her power over the men to make them spare the church, in which the frightened inhabitants had stored most of their goods.

Now she desired greatly to march on Paris, but this the King would not hear of, and she was sent to besiege La Charité, a town of considerable strength. The army was badly equipped, and ill-furnished with munition of war. The Court either could not or would not supply them, and Joan wrote to several towns, begging them for arms and other necessaries. Her letter to the town of Riom still exists, the signature in her own hand—her hand guided probably by the secretary. Many places sent contributions, but not enough to carry on the siege, and by the end of November it had to be given up.

Joan returned to the Court, where she was honourably received, the King not blaming her for the failure before La Charité, nor his councillors bearing her any grudge for it. Indeed it was by failure she could best please them. The King, in acknowledgment of her great services, ennobled her, her family, and all their legitimate descendants for ever. She had already received armorial bearings in which figured the lilies of France, and now her brothers, who were quick to grasp at the new honours, took the surname of Du Lis. But she, whose simple nobleness no King could increase, kept her own name and her own banner, showing a silent disregard for worthless honours—worthless, because they betokened no real gratitude nor trust.

About this time Charles and his council were inclined to let a mock prophetess share or rival the Maid's honour. This woman, Catherine of Rochelle, was received by the King, whom she informed that a white lady, clothed all in gold, came to her every night, and bade her go with royal heralds from city

G

to city, commanding the people to bring out their money for the payment of Joan's army. The King's advisers were half-willing to make use of Catherine, and were encouraged to do so by Friar Richard, whom she thoroughly deceived. The credulous preacher tried to make Joan accept this new ally, and Joan, doubting her, yet wishing to be just, shared her bed for a night to watch for the white lady. After some hours the Maid fell asleep, and in the morning was told by Catherine that the vision had come and gone. Joan slept in the day, so as to keep awake all the next night; as she lay watching, she asked from time to time, " Will she not come ?" and Catherine answered, " Yes, presently." But the white lady never came, and Joan advised the would-be seer, who was married, to go home and mind her house. Catherine's inspiration was not of the warlike sort. She declined going to the siege of La Charité because of the cold, but wished to be sent in state to negotiate with the Duke of Burgundy. Joan told her, with some scorn doubtless, that peace with Burgundy was to be won only at the point of the lance.

After the affair of La Charité, Joan spent four weary months—how weary, we conjecture chiefly from what we know of her character and her aspirations, for there is but slight record of the time. Occasionally she rode with a few followers to visit some town where she was known, but generally she was with the Court, a sad and unwilling spectator of its festivities. Sad only because of her unfulfilled mission: had she been suffered to work it out, to see France delivered, she would doubtless have lived like other women of her rank, and taken a woman's pleasure in show and gaiety. For she was at home and happy with noble knights and ladies, and took a frank delight in rich garments and fine armour. She was no bigot. Her sanctity was altogether wholesome : it was an exalted love for God, for France and the King, unsoured by any contempt for the common life of humanity.

Wherever she went she visited the sick, she gave all she could in alms, she was devoted to the services of the Church and to prayer. The people, who knew of her greatness and saw her goodness, treated her with a reverence that was akin to superstition. They brought rings and crosses for her to touch, and so turn into amulets. " Touch them yourselves," she would say, laughing, " they will be just as good." Some believed that she had a charmed life, and need never fear going into battle.

The truce with Burgundy had been extended to Easter, and Pont St. Maxence given as a pledge to the Duke. He would have preferred Compiègne, a place of far greater importance, and the King would have given it, but its inhabitants refused to allow the transfer. Philip tried to buy it from Guillaume de Flavy, the governor; but De Flavy, though a man of many crimes, was staunch to the King, and would not be bribed. Then the Duke, determined to have the town, made up his mind to hold with the English, and got ready to aid them in driving Charles out of the Isle-of-France.

News of his preparations, with other news, some hopeful, some disheartening, came to the Maid at Sully, where Charles was again the guest of La Tremouille. She heard of La Hire's success in Normandy, where he had taken Louviers and Château Gaillard, and rescued the brave leader, Barbazan, from captivity. She heard, probably, of the plot in favour of Charles which was then being matured in Paris, a plot that was soon found out and cruelly repressed. She heard also of the imminent arrival of Henry the Sixth, of the misery that was in the Isle-of-France, and the terror of its loyal cities. The people of Reims, who had special cause for fear, sent to tell her of their danger, and on March 16th, 1430, she wrote to comfort them :—

"Dear and well-beloved, whom I greatly desire to see, Joan the Maid has received your letters making mention that you fear a siege. Know that you shall have none if I can meet them, but if, before I meet them, they come against you, shut your gates; for I will come to you shortly, and make them want their spurs in such haste that they shall not know where to find them ; and their destruction shall be quick and soon. I can write no more to you now, except that you do remain always good and loyal. I pray God to have you in his keeping.

"I could send you other news that would greatly rejoice you, but I fear the letters might be taken on the way, and the news read.—JEHANNE."

Not only were there enemies outside Reims : there was also the fear of traitors within its gates. Joan received a second letter from its inhabitants, and on the 28th, wrote again, assuring them of the King's favour, and promising them his help. She was eager to carry it to them. Though there is no account of her pleadings, we who know her know how she must have implored the King to let her go and save the threatened province. But the truce was not yet over, and Charles, lapped in the delights of Sully, would not anticipate by an hour the day of needful action.

Joan grew desperate. Sad voices from beyond the Loire were calling her. She was greatly wanted there, and the King—her King whom she had crowned—did not want her, cared nothing for her nor for his people's trouble. She asked counsel of her other voices, of her saints, and they neither bade her go nor stay; they told her only one certain thing, that before St. John's Day she would be taken. If so—if indeed, as she herself had said, she was to last only a year—then the more need to hasten with her work. One day at the end of March she left Sully with a small company, as if going for one of her usual rides. She did not bid farewell to the King, and she never saw him again.

CHAPTER VI.

CAPTIVITY.

JOAN and her little company rode towards Paris. She was at Melun in Easter week, and at the expiration of the truce went to Lagny-sur-Marne, "because those of the place had fought the English well at Paris and elsewhere." While there, she led a sally against Franquet d'Arras, a Burgundian knight, who had been ravaging the country with a band of freebooters. Franquet was taken, and Joan would have treated him as a prisoner of war, but the civil authorities claimed him as a robber, murderer, and traitor, and after due trial he was condemned and executed.

She had a gentler memory than this to take with her from Lagny. A baby, three days old and unbaptised, was lying as if dead, and would have been buried in unconsecrated ground; but some young girls of the place carried it before the altar of the Virgin, and besought God to restore it to life, if only for a moment, that it might be received into the Church. They begged Joan to go with them, and she did so. While they were praying, the child moved, a natural colour came into its face, and it lived long enough to be baptised. Many people believed that Joan had restored it by a miracle.

By the end of April, the Duke of Burgundy had taken the field, and attacked the fortresses about Compiègne. Joan arrived there on May 13th, and found the Count of Vendôme and the Archbishop of Reims within the city, the latter perhaps still thinking to treat with Philip. Philip was now besieging Choisi-sur-Aisne, and Joan led an expedition to relieve it, but was repulsed at the passage of the Oise. She next tried to reach it by crossing the Aisne at Soissons, but the traitorous governor of the place refused to let the troops pass, and almost immediately afterwards admitted a party of Burgundians. Choisi was soon taken and destroyed.

Joan returned to Compiègne, dispirited by her failure, bewildered at the treachery she had just witnessed. It was a time of sad forebodings for her. A story goes, that one morning, after hearing mass in the church of St. Jacques, she went apart and leaned dejectedly against a pillar. Some grown people and a crowd of children came about her—she was always gentle to children—and she said to them, "My children and dear friends, I tell you that I am sold and betrayed, and that I shall soon be given up to death. Therefore I entreat you to pray for me, for never again shall I have any power to serve the King or the Kingdom of France." She was not "sold and betrayed" yet; that was to come.

Depression could not make her inactive. She went to Crespy for reinforcements, but hearing that the siege of Compiègne had begun, she hurried back there on the night of the 23rd, with about four hundred men. She entered the place at sunrise, and spent the chief part of the day in arranging a sortie, to be made before evening. Compiègne, situated on the south bank of the Oise, was connected with the opposite shore by a bridge, from which a raised causeway went over the low river-meadows to the hill-slopes of Picardy. At the end of this causeway was the village of Margny, now held by the Burgundians; west of it was Venette, occupied by the English; John of Luxembourg and his Picards were at Clairoix, to the north-east; and the Duke himself, with a reserve force, was at Caudun, a league to the north, on the little river Aronde. Joan's plan was, to drive the Burgundians from Margny, pursue them to Clairoix, and there fall upon John of Luxembourg's men, while a party from Compiègne was to hold the bridge and causeway, so as to keep the English from coming to help their allies. Guillaume de Flavy had boats also ready on the Oise, to further a retreat, if necessary.

Late in the afternoon, Joan, with five hundred foot and horsemen, charged down on Margny, and drove the Burgundians into the meadow east of the causeway. But John of Luxembourg happened to be with them, and he sent in haste to Clairoix for his Picards. This reinforcement caused the French to be outnumbered; still they fought with some success, until the English came up, as had been foreseen, to attack the causeway. Then Joan's troops forgot or distrusted its defenders. They feared to be cut off from Compiègne, to be left in a country dotted with the enemy's camps, and most of them turned, panic-stricken, and fled towards the city.

The English gained the causeway, and the archers stationed there dared not shoot on them for fear of hurting their own people. The guns of Compiègne were useless, for friends and foes were mingled in a confused struggle. Joan tried to rally her men : " Hold your peace !" she cried to some who spoke of retreating. "It depends on you to discomfit them ! Think only of falling upon them !" But her words were in vain. All she could do was to cover the retreat, and that she did valiantly, riding last, and charging back often. Thanks to her, a great part of the fugitives got safely into the city, while others reached the boats ; but the English pressed towards the gate to cut off the retreat of the remainder, and Guillaume de Flavy, afraid, as he said, lest in the

confusion they might rush into the town itself,
ordered the drawbridge to be raised, and the port-
cullis lowered. There was no escape for the Maid
now. She and a little devoted band that kept with
her fought desperately, but they were driven into an
angle of the fortifications, and soon surrounded.
Jean d'Aulon, Poton de Saintrailles, and her brother
Pierre were taken prisoners; many fell in defending
her.

Compiègne remained shut. The city to whose help
she had come at dawn saw her lost at its very gates
before sundown, and made no effort to save her.
Five or six men rushed on her at once, each crying,
"Yield to me! Pledge your faith to me!" "I have
sworn and pledged my faith to another than you,"
she said, "and I will keep my oath." She still struck
at those who tried to seize her; but an archer came
behind her, and, grasping the gold-embroidered sur-
coat that she wore, dragged her from her horse. She
fell, exhausted and overcome at last, and the man who
had pulled her down carried her to his master, the
bastard of Wandomme, a vassal of John of Luxembourg.

She was taken to Margny, and thither flocked the
English and Burgundian captains, "more joyful than
if they had taken five hundred fighting men." In
this very month of her capture, it had been found
needful to issue proclamations against English

soldiers, men of the old conquering race, who had
refused to come over to France for fear of the Witch.
And now here was the Witch, vanquished, powerless,
her armour soiled in the fight, her magic banner
fallen away from her.   The chiefs could hardly
believe their good fortune, but her sad presence was
there to assure them of it, and they came and gazed
on her.   Among them came the Duke of Burgundy,
who had got news of the skirmish too late to take
part in it.   He spoke to the Maid, and she to him,
but we have no record of the interview, though
Philip's secretary, the historian Monstrelet, was
present at it.   When she chose, Joan could speak
sharp words of reproof, and such words she doubtless
had for the man whom she had vainly entreated to
spare his country, and save it from the dominion of
strangers.

For three or four days she was kept at Margny,
longing, hoping for a rescue, expecting it perhaps
from hour to hour.   John of Luxembourg, to whom
she was now transferred, had some groundless fear of
the same thing, and therefore he sent her to his castle
of Beaulieu, a short distance from Compiègne.
Before her removal, the news of her capture had gone
through France.   On May 25th they reached Paris,
where Bedford caused *Te Deums* to be sung in all
the churches.   Next day the University and the
Vicar of the Inquisition wrote to the Duke of

Burgundy, whose vassal John of Luxembourg was, requiring him to give Joan up to ecclesiastical justice. The Duke took no notice of those letters. He had his own advantage to consult, his own terms to make, and it might be for his advantage to surrender the Maid to Charles. He half-expected Charles, with all French France at his back, to claim her with threats or promises, to ransom her royally, or come more royally yet with an army to tear her from her captors. John of Luxembourg, who also had his own interests to look to, absolutely refused to give her up for any demand of University or Inquisitor. Neither of them wished to bring upon himself the scorn and hatred of the country, so they both bided their time.

How did Joan's friends, those whom she had raised up and delivered, receive the news of her sorrow? The populace heard of it first with unbelief, then with ready anger against the nobles, who, they declared, had betrayed her to her enemies. The towns that knew her paid her their tribute of mourning. She was prayed for in the churches, and at Tours a procession of bare-footed priests implored heaven for her deliverance. Useless and fruitless signs of grief! In all the cities there was no one found to go to her help. Among all the captains who had been with her in the good days of victory, not one thought of leading his men to Beaulieu, and rescuing her from her prison.

And Charles? Gratitude, that rare virtue in princes, was utterly unknown to him, the king of false courtiers and greedy sycophants. His thanklessness almost passes belief. He made no effort, wrote no line, expressed no desire for Joan's deliverance. He did absolutely nothing. We have no record of even a regretful word, a sorrowful look from him when he heard of her captivity. To his courtiers that captivity was no matter for regret. They had always been jealous of her. Even those who had been half-friendly to her felt relieved now to have her out of the way; she had so often vexed them with her straightforward boldness, her unwavering trust in Heaven, her grand scorn for their intrigues and negotiations and underhand ways. Regnault de Chartres wrote to the people of Reims, telling of her misfortune, which he considered a judgment from Heaven, "because she would not hear counsel, but did everything according to her own pleasure." However, her loss mattered little, for "there was come to the King a young shepherd from the mountains of Gévaudan, who said neither more nor less than Joan had done, that he had God's command to go with the King's army, and certainly the English and Burgundians should be discomfited." The shepherd further declared that God had permitted Joan's downfall, "because she had given way to pride, and worn rich garments, and did not follow His commandment, nor do His will." This wretched parody on the Maid was indeed employed with the royal troops, and after about a year was taken by the English and thrown into the Seine.

Philip and his vassal heard doubtless of the Archbishop's letter, and judged from it how little Charles and his council cared what became of Joan. No offer for her ransom, no threats of vengeance, came from beyond the Loire; but there were good offers from the English, and strong inducements to give her up existed north of the Seine. The Duke of Brabant was dying, and Philip would get possession of his duchy; but there was small chance of his keeping it, unless by treaties with England he could insure commercial prosperity to its towns. John of Luxembourg had also an inheritance to secure. He belonged to an illustrious race, but he was poor, and his poverty was at strife with his honour.

From the first moment of Joan's captivity, Bedford had been anxious to get her into his power. He feared that Philip might be persuaded to give her back to her party, that John of Luxembourg might be bribed with a town or a province—for what would the King not do to save her who had almost saved his kingdom? The Regent made no attempt to claim her as a prisoner of war. As such, the laws of war would protect her, and her

ransom once paid, she could not in justice be detained
a single day. Nor did he demand her as a rebel
against Henry; for she was that no more than any
other person who had fought for Charles. Rebels, in
such circumstances, *were* prisoners of war, and no
captivity, however long, would be punishment enough
for the Witch. Death must be her reward, and a
death so bitter, so shameful, as amply to avenge the
English, and throw all possible discredit on her and
on her mission. The Church, by its appeal to
Burgundy, had shown him how to secure his end, and
to the Church Bedford went for assistance.

There was an instrument ready to his hand, one
well fitted by nature and circumstance to be the
unjust judge of a helpless woman : a churchman of
great learning, great ambition, and no scruples ; a
friend of Burgundy, an influential member of the
University of Paris. This was Pierre Cauchon, that
Bishop of Beauvais who had been driven out of his city
at Joan's victorious approach. He had found a refuge
in England; and when the Cardinal of Winchester
came to France with the young king, Cauchon came
in his train, hoping perhaps that English victories
might reinstate him in his diocese. But a grander
bait was held out for his fidelity. The See of Rouen
was vacant, and Winchester half-promised that he
would persuade the Pope to bestow it on him. The
task proposed to Cauchon was much to his taste.

While securing his own promotion, he could be revenged on the girl who had in a manner robbed him of his bishopric, and through her could injure the hated Armagnac party. He set to work at once, supported zealously by the University of Paris, and approved by the Inquisition.

But before he could try Joan, he had to get possession of her. He was still Bishop of Beauvais, and the meadow-land where she had been taken happened to be within that diocese ; therefore she was his to judge for any faults committed against the Church. On July 14th, he went to the camp before Compiègne, and claimed her as a witch, idolatress, and heretic. He took with him letters from the University ; he took also offers of money from the English Regent. The Duke and his vassals still put off surrendering the Maid. Perhaps some feeling of knightly honour held them back ; perhaps they were expecting better offers from Charles. Now was his time ; now was the time for the good cities to collect a ransom, and buy Joan's freedom and her gracious presence with the royal army. But the weeks went by, and no one stirred to help her. Her captors' scruples were overcome, and before winter she was bought and sold. John of Luxembourg got ten thousand livres. Philip, who by this time had inherited Brabant, was secured in it by the friendship of England

II

During the summer months Joan was kept at Beaulieu, with her good Jean d'Aulon to attend her. He, though a captive also, had tidings from without, and could tell her of victories won by the French, and also of the great danger of Compiègne. " That poor city that you have loved so much must fall into the hands of the enemies of France." " Not so," she answered, " for none of the places that the King of Heaven has restored to the good King Charles by my means shall be taken by his enemies so long as he is diligent to keep them." One day she tried to escape, and had actually locked her jailors into the keep, but the porter saw her, and took her back. Early in August she was sent to Beaurevoir, a stronger castle, and farther from the seat of war. John of Luxembourg's wife, and his aunt, the aged Countess of Ligny, lived there, and they treated Joan with much kindness. They offered her female attire, begging her to leave off the man's dress she wore, but she refused. " I can quit it only with my Lord's will," she said, "and the time is not come yet." The dress seemed to her a token of future liberty, of more work to be done for France.

The ladies were won by her simple goodness, by her piety, by the proud modesty with which she repelled the over-free advances of some of the young nobles about the castle. They heard with indignation of Cauchon's overtures to John of Luxembourg, and they knelt at their lord's feet, imploring him not to disgrace his name and his knighthood by selling the Maid to her enemies. They must have told Joan of their anxiety, for she knew what bargaining was going on. She knew also that Compiègne was hard pressed, and that Philip had threatened to put to death all its inhabitants over seven years of age. Through her own worst grief, her sympathy with the grief of others remained quick and keen. Towards every city she had won for Charles she felt most kindly affection, as towards a home. The news caused her an agony of sorrow. "How shall God let those good people die, who have been, and are so loyal to their lord ?" she exclaimed. She forgot how disloyal Compiègne had been to her. Oh, if she could but go to save it, to raise the siege as she had done at Orleans! Her saints had sent her there ; would they not send her to this city also ? In the solitude of her prison she called upon her voices, and entreated them to let her go.

She was allowed upon the ramparts to take the air, but never to go into the court-yard of the castle, and her prison-room was in the upper part of a high tower, and carefully guarded. Sixty feet of straight wall, sixty feet of empty air, were between her and freedom. If her saints would help her—would bear her up in their hands, she might cast herself safely through that terrible space. She told them of her thought, but the *voices* blamed her for it. They bade her wait, for she would be delivered, but not until she had seen the King of England. They told her to have patience, for God would save Compiègne. Wait? Have patience?—and she was being chaffered for at that very moment, and Compiègne was on the very point of being taken! She would not see the English King! She would rather die than fall into English hands! For the first time, she rebelled against her voices.

She knotted together strips of stuff—probably the bed-furniture of her cell—and let herself down, commending herself to God and the Virgin. But the frail line broke, and presently she was found lying senseless at the foot of the tower. They who raised her thought she must be dead, but she soon revived, and she had no bone broken, nor any lasting injury. For three days she lay, unable to eat or drink, listening to her voices, that rebuked and comforted her. They bade her confess, and ask God's pardon for her want of faith, and they again promised her that Compiègne should be delivered before the winter.

The place was hemmed in, much as Orleans had been, by forts and boulevards, so that the people, unable to get any supplies, were almost reduced to famine. But on October 25th, an army led by the Count of Vendôme went to their relief, and, owing to a mistake of John of Luxembourg, succeeded in forcing three of his bastiles. The Anglo-Burgundians were utterly discouraged. Many of them deserted during the night, and the next day, to the amazement of the French, the siege was raised, and the besiegers retired, leaving behind them all their artillery and a great quantity of spoil.

But this rescue that Joan had longed and prayed for hastened her own ruin. John of Luxembourg now wanted money more than ever, and his defeat had moreover embittered him against the French party. About the middle of November he finally sold the Maid. She was taken first to Arras, then to Crotoy, where she was given up to the English, who, as an old chronicle says, "were more rejoiced than if they had gained all the gold of Lombardy." She was kept at Crotoy until the place of her trial was settled, and was not hardly treated, being allowed to hear mass, and even to receive some visitors. Several ladies of Abbeville came to see her, and were touched by her youth, her gentleness and sorrow. They wept at parting from her, and she kissed them as she said farewell, entreating them to remember her in their prayers.

No sooner had the University heard of the final surrender of the Maid, than it wrote to congratulate Henry, its "dread and sovereign lord and master," and advised him to have her tried in Paris. It wrote also to Cauchon, urging the same thing, and blaming

him sharply for his lack of zeal in not having already
brought her to justice. It is not unlikely that both
those letters were written at Cauchon's instigation, so
as to take some of the responsibility of the trial off
his own shoulders.

But Bedford had no intention of sending Joan back
to the debated land of the Isle-of-France, where even
Paris was no sure possession. Its people were sick of
trouble and scarcity. They avowedly disliked their
foreign masters, and were discontented with the Duke
of Burgundy, who had not been near them for a
twelvemonth, and "cared nothing if they suffered
thirst or hunger." Who could tell what reaction
might be caused by Joan's presence among them,
even as a prisoner? Rouen, in the centre of the
English power, in a country where she was comparatively little known, was chosen for the place of
her trial, and she was brought there late in December,
1430.

Nearly two months were spent in preparing for the
trial. The Chapter of Rouen had been very unwilling
to give Cauchon the territorial letters, without which
he could hold no authority within the diocese, and it at
last only granted them under compulsion (December
28th). The prelate then set to work to find fitting
colleagues. He first chose about forty assessors, six
of them doctors from the University of Paris, the rest
scholars and churchmen, obedient, or at least

favourable, to the English. With three exceptions, they were all Frenchmen. If the odium of buying the Maid, of holding her in dreadful bondage, and putting her to a cruel death, rests with the English, that of selling her, of judging her unjustly, and torturing while they judged her, must remain with her own country-people to their everlasting shame.

A few of those whom the Bishop had selected turned against the task set before them ; but they were all cajoled or frightened into submission, except Nicolas de Houppeville, who with noble courage declared the proceedings illegal, not only because the chief judge was an enemy of the accused, but also because he had no right to try over again one who had already been tried and approved of by his metropolitan, the Archbishop of Reims. The bold dissentient spoke at the risk of his life. Cauchon imprisoned him, and threatened to have him drowned, but some of his friends got him away and out of Rouen.

On January 3rd, a letter written in Henry's name gave the Maid up to her judges, at the same time stipulating that if the Church acquitted her, she must still remain a prisoner to the English. On the 9th, Cauchon assembled a few of his assessors, to explain the reasons for the trial, and appoint officers to serve on it. For promoter or proctor-general he chose Jean d'Estivet, who had been his vicar-general at

Beauvais, and had shared his banishment ; Jean de la
Fontaine was made commissioner ; Guillaume Colles
and Guillaume Manchon were appointed scribes or
reporters ; and Jean Massieu, usher of the court.

As the trial was to be conducted after the forms of
the Inquisition, and as the Holy Office required to
have minute knowledge of the antecedents of those
offenders with whom it had to deal, Joan's past life
was most carefully investigated. The Duchess of
Bedford deputed two matrons of Rouen to see her in
prison and pronounce as to her chastity, and commissioners were sent to her native place to make the
closest inquiries about her. Every report was in her
favour. The commissioners did their work con-
scientiously, and had only good to tell of her. One
of them, Nicolas Bailly, assured Cauchon that he had
heard nothing about her which he would not gladly
have found in his own sister. The Bishop was
furious with this over-honest agent ; he reviled him as
a traitor, a bringer of worthless information, and at
first refused to pay the cost of the inquiry.

On the 13th, and again on the 23rd of January,
Cauchon called together six churchmen, to whom he
gave a more or less exact version of Bailly's report.
They decided, for the sake of clearness and brevity,
to condense it into a certain number of articles, which
should guide the court in its examination of the
accused. A larger council was called on February

13th, when the officers of the trial were formally sworn ; and six days later was held the last pre-liminary meeting, at which the vice-inquisitor, Jean Lemaître, objected to assist in the proceedings, stating that his commission was only for the diocese of Rouen, and therefore he could not lawfully meddle with the affairs of Beauvais. The Inquisition had no great power in France, but a trial for heresy unsupported by it would have been little respected in the south of Europe. Cauchon, who had promised to get up "a fine trial," was resolved to have its countenance. He procured letters from the chief inquisitor for France, setting aside his deputy's ingenious plea, and ordering him to act. Until those letters came, Jean Lemaître attended as an assessor.

Our knowledge of the trial is derived, not from contemporary chronicles, which either ignore it alto-gether, or mention it in the slightest way, but chiefly from the judicial reports of each day's proceedings. These reports were taken on the spot by the scribe Manchon, and it is from him and from other witnesses at the trial of atonement that we have extra-judicial details of Joan's life and manner of bearing herself during this time. Manchon's real desire to act fairly by the accused brought on him the frequent anger of her judges. He was warned by some of them that he must not always report her exact words, and was often forbidden to write down answers of hers that displeased the Bishop. His notes, after being compared with those of the other scribes, and submitted to official inspection, were copied on the evening of each day under his own supervision ; but as he wrote in French, and Latin was then the language of jurisprudence, they were afterwards translated by Thomas de Courcelles. De Courcelles, a famous scholar and able upholder of the rights of the Gallican Church, was the youngest of all the assessors, and the most coldly stern.

But a small portion of the original record remains to us, and both that and the Latin version we must read with a certain distrust. Manchon, however honest and well-meaning, must have somewhat deferred to the Bishop, otherwise he would have suffered for his contumacy, or, at the very least, would have been dismissed from his office of scribe. In Courcelles' version, even supposing it tolerably faithful, we lose much of the power and freshness of the original French. We long to have the very words that came warm and living from Joan's lips. Still, through all obscurities and perversions, we see, though as in a glass darkly, the noble figure of the Maid, and are taught to love and honour her by the story of her martyrdom left to us by her most bitter enemies.

CHAPTER VII.

THE EXAMINATION IN COURT.

HITHERTO we have seen Joan, a gracious figure always—better always and nobler than her surroundings—but never yet solitary in goodness and nobleness. Other figures have been grouped about her, gracious also in their degree, worthy to divide with her our sympathy, and to have some share in our love. Now they are all gone from her. Father and mother, village friends and kinsfolk, devoted comrades and adoring people, are all shut away from her for ever. The old life is over. With the new year a new and dreadful life has begun for her, a torturing of mind and body, a long monotony of anguish. Taking into account the youth, the sex, and the innocence of the victim, her pitiful tragedy has no parallel in history.

She is desolate, and worse than alone; to the darling of the saints, loneliness would be no such terrible punishment. Wrong and horror crowd upon her. Her honour and her life are in the hands of men evil by nature, or turned to evil by hatred, or greed, or fear.   Here and there a judge speaks some word in favour of banished justice, but those feeble flashes leave no light in the gloom.   The light shines all on Joan.   The pure maiden, the noble heroine, stands out, heaven-illumined, against the darkness. Her sorrow and her endurance of it crown and sanctify her.   Piteous though her fate be, we almost forget to pity her, for compassion is well-nigh lost in reverence and wonder.

On her arrival at Rouen, Joan was taken to the castle, and put into an iron cage that had been made to receive her; and, as if its bars were not enough, she was chained in it by her neck, her hands, and her feet. After being kept thus for several days, she was transferred to a gloomy chamber in one of the towers, where she was fettered to a great log of wood during the day, and to her bed at night.   Both by night and day, she was guarded by five English soldiers of the lowest and rudest class, three of whom were always with her, while the other two kept the door outside. The perpetual presence of such watchers would have been a horror and an insult to the vilest of women : let us remember what Joan was—how jealously she guarded her purity—how among men-at-arms she had kept the delicacy of her womanhood—and we shall understand a little of the hourly misery she had to suffer.

Once given over to the Church, she should have been placed in an ecclesiastical prison, and guarded by women. For this right she pleaded often, and her plea was supported by several of the assessors. But the English would not lose their grip of a captive who had cost them and lost them so much, and Pierre Cauchon had too great fear of displeasing them to advise such a simple measure of decency and justice.

Joan had visitors in her prison. English nobles, whose nobility did not keep them from insulting a woman and a helpless captive, came to stare and jest at her. Warwick and Stafford came one day, and with them a man who might well have shrunk from looking her in the face—the Judas of Luxembourg. He told her he had come to ransom her, on condition that she would not again take up arms against England. She answered him scornfully, as he deserved : "In God's name, you but mock me, for I know you have neither the will nor the power to do it;" and she added, "I know that the English will kill me, thinking to have the kingdom of France after my death ; but were they a hundred thousand *Goddams* more than they are, they should not have the kingdom." Hereupon Lord Stafford drew his dagger upon her, but Warwick held him back.

Whatever might be the issue of the trial, the English were resolved that there must be but one

end for Joan.   So long as she lived, she would make
cowards of their best soldiers.   Even in prison she
was strong, for who could know with what holy
prayers or unholy spells she might be helping her
cause?   Who but she had raised the siege of Compiègne?   Who but she was even now aiding Vendôme
and Brabazan and La Hire?   La Hire occupied
Louviers, but a short distance from Rouen, and
thence came out and pillaged safely, for the English
would hardly try to dislodge him so long as Joan
lived.   Some impatient spirits would have ended her
troubles and their own ill-luck by throwing her into
the Seine, but those violent ones, like Stafford, were
too hasty and too merciful.

According to Massieu's testimony (given at the
trial of atonement), Cauchon refused the Maid's just
request for counsel to advise and defend her during
her examination.   But he was not merciful enough to
leave her to the guidance of her own wise brain and
true heart.   According to the bad custom of the
Inquisition, he sent her a sham confidant, a creature
even more abject than himself—his friend and tool,
the Canon Loyseleur.   This man went to Joan in dis-
guise, and told her that he too was a prisoner, a loyal
subject of King Charles, and a native of her own province.   The guards, with suspicious kindness, left
them together, and she, poor child, being glad to see a
friendly face, talked to him with a trustfulness that

might have touched even such a heart as his. The Bishop listened in an adjoining room, and stationed two scribes there to report Joan's words; but the men were too honest for such work, and refused to do it. To gain her fuller confidence, Loyseleur made known to her that he was a priest, and heard her in confession. He also gave her counsel how to answer her judges—bad and crooked counsel, of which she availed herself little, but still enough for us to trace here and there the influence of an evil mind over hers.

On Tuesday, February 20th, she was summoned to appear next day before her judges. Having heard and seen what they were, she demanded that an equal number of assessors of the French party should be associated with them. She also entreated Cauchon to let her hear mass, for since her departure from Crotoy she had been at no religious service. The demand was simply ignored; the prayer was denied.

At eight o'clock on Wednesday morning, the Bishop, his officers, and forty-two assessors met in the chapel of the castle. When certain preliminaries had been gone through, Joan was sent for, and appeared before them a youthful, girlish creature in her masculine dress. The dress was all black, relieved only by the pale prison-worn face, from which the dark eyes looked out fearlessly.

The Bishop began by briefly stating the crimes she

was accused of, and explaining to her how he came
to be her judge. He then exhorted her, "with gentleness and charity," to answer truly all questions put
to her, both for the speedy despatch of the business in
hand, and for the relief of her own conscience. From
the first moment of the trial she was on her guard.
She who had replied so freely and readily to the
doctors at Poitiers, now answered with the cautious-
ness of distrust. There, under all the gruffness and
sternness of her examiners, she had felt their real
desire for truth; here, she felt her judges' falsehood
and malevolence in the very air around her.

The Gospels were brought, and she was ordered to
swear upon them that she would speak the truth.
She hesitated : " I do not know what questions you
may put to me," she said ; " perhaps you will ask me
things I cannot tell you."

" Will you swear," insisted Cauchon, " to speak the
truth about whatever you are asked concerning the
faith, and whatever you know ?" She answered that
she would willingly speak of her parents, and of all
her own actions since she had left Domremy. " But
as for the revelations from God, I have never spoken
of them except to King Charles, my lord, and I will
not reveal them, even though my head were to be cut
off, for my *counsel* has told me not to speak of them.
Nevertheless, within a week I shall know whether I
may reveal them." Her words were interrupted by a

tumult of questions and contradictions, everyone speaking at once. There was a noisy debate about the oath, and at last she was persuaded to take it, with reservations as to her visions. Kneeling, and with her hands on the Gospels, she swore to speak truly on matters of faith.

She was first questioned about her name, her birth-place and parentage, her baptism and her religious knowledge. " My mother taught me Our Father," she said, " the Hail Mary, the Belief; it is from my mother that I hold my belief." As was usual in inquisitorial trials, she was told to repeat the Lord's Prayer, but she refused to do so except in confession.

Before dismissing her for that day, Cauchon forbade her to attempt escaping, under penalty of being reputed a heretic. " I do not accept your prohibition," she replied. " Were I to escape, no one could reproach me with having broken faith, for I have pledged it to no one." She complained of her chains, and the Bishop told her they were considered necessary, because she had already tried to escape. " It is true," she answered, " that I have desired and do desire to escape. That is lawful for every prisoner." She was given in strict charge to three English guards, who were sworn on the Gospels to let no one have access to her, and was cited to appear again next morning before the tribunal.

Because of the unseemly confusion of the first day's

I

proceedings, Cauchon resolved to hold his court thenceforth, not in the chapel, but in a room adjoining the great hall of the castle. To reach this hall, Joan had to pass the chapel, and as Massieu was leading her by the door, she stopped, saying, "Is not the body of Christ there?" and persuaded him to let her kneel a moment and pray. Jean d'Estivet found this out, and abused the kind-hearted usher, threatening that if he transgressed again he should be put where he would see neither moon nor stars for a month. The promoter, petty as most cruel natures are, used afterwards to await Joan's coming, and stand between her and the chapel door, to keep her from even approaching it.

Cauchon opened the second day's business by requiring her to swear unconditionally that she would tell the whole truth; but she held out against his persuasions, and finally was allowed to take the same oath as on the day before. Her examination was committed to Jean Beaupère, who gently exhorted her to answer faithfully, "according to her oath." She saw the trap he was laying for her. "You might ask me some things about which I could tell you the truth," she said, "and others about which I could not tell it." Then she added, "If you were well informed about me, you would wish me out of your hands. I have done nothing except by revelation."

She spoke excitedly, and, to calm her, Beaupère led

her to speak of her home and her youth. By degrees he drew her on to more dangerous ground. He asked her if she had been used to confess regularly. " Yes," she said, " to my priest ; and when he was prevented, to some other, with his leave. Sometimes, twice or thrice, I think, I confessed to mendicant friars ; it was at Neufchâteau. I used to communicate at Easter."

" And at other feasts ? "

" Pass that over." *Pass that over* was her usual answer when the examiner's probe touched any subject she counted too secret or too sacred for discussion.

He questioned her next about her revelations, and she told him as much as she had told to many others, and no more. She spoke frankly of the light that had appeared to her ; of the voices that had sent her into France ; of her own unwillingness and fears ; of her appeals to Baudricourt, her journey to Chinon, and her recognition of the King. Her judges were very curious to know what mysterious *sign* she had given to Charles. She was asked if, when her voices showed her the King, the usual light appeared to her. She answered, " Pass that over."

" Did you see an angel above your King's head ? "

" I pray you, pass that over ! "

They extorted from her that before the King agreed to employ her he had beautiful revelations, but when asked what they were, she said, " I will not tell you ; this is not the time to answer. Send to the King, and he will tell them to you." Further questioning drew from her that her own party believed her voices were from God ; that the voices came to her every day—she had great need of them, she added pathetically ; that she had never asked them for any reward except the salvation of her soul.

The attack on Paris was the next subject of investigation. Yes, she said, she had commanded it, and she would have renewed it after her failure, but she was forced to leave St. Denis against the counsel of her voices.

"Was not the attack on a feast-day?" she was asked. She answered that she believed so.

"And was that right?" She refused to answer the question. "Pass that over," she said. Here the day's examination ended, and Saturday was appointed for the next meeting of the court.

Six new assessors had joined it on Thursday, and on Saturday came thirteen more, raising their number to sixty-three. The Bishop again charged Joan to take an absolute and unconditional oath. "Let me speak," she pleaded. "By my faith, you might ask me things I could not tell you ! Perhaps I could not speak truly about many things you would ask me— such as my revelations. You might force me to reveal what I have sworn not to reveal, and so I should perjure myself, and that you ought not to

wish." The Bishop still insisted, threatening probably
to use his authority as her judge, and she spoke more
vehemently : " I tell you, take heed how you say you
are my judge ; for you take too much upon yourself,
and you lay too much on me. Methinks it is enough
to have sworn twice."

Cauchon asked if she would let herself be advised
by some of those present whether to answer or no. " I
will tell the truth about my coming to France," she
said, "and nothing further. You must ask me no
more." He persevered, telling her that by refusing to
swear, she exposed herself to suspicion of guilt. She
grew weary of his importunity. " I come from God,"
she cried, "and I have nothing to do here. Send me
back to God, from whom I come!" The Bishop then
required her to swear that she would answer truly in
all that concerned her trial, and that oath she took
without further objections.

Jean Beaupère now took up the examination. His
first question was, when had she last eaten and drunk.
It was the season of Lent ; if she had taken food as
usual, she might be accused of contempt for the
Church ; if she had fasted, she gave colour to a
theory of Beaupère's, that her visions were induced
chiefly by physical causes. She told him she had
fasted since noon the day before. He inquired at
what hour she had last heard the *voice*. " I heard it
yesterday and to-day," she said. " I was asleep, and

it woke me. . . . I do not know whether it was in my room, but it was in the castle. . . . I thanked it, sitting up in my bed, with clasped hands, and implored its counsel. . . . I had asked God to teach me by its counsel how to answer."

"And what did the voice say?"

"It told me to answer boldly, and God would help me." Here she turned to the Bishop. "You say that you are my judge. Take heed what you do, for indeed I am sent by God, and you are putting yourself in great peril."

Beaupère asked her if the voice never varied in its counsel. "No," she said; "it has never contradicted itself. Last night again it bade me answer boldly." He then asked whether she had been forbidden to answer unreservedly on her trial, and to tell her revelations. She refused to answer those questions without leave from her *counsel*, which to her meant leave from God; for she said, "I believe firmly, as firmly as I believe the Christian faith, and that God died to save us from the pains of hell, that the voices come from Him." She was asked whether the voice was that of an angel or of a saint, or of God Himself. "The voice comes from God," she repeated. "I do not tell you all I know, for I fear more to err by saying anything that might offend those voices than I fear to fail in answering you. I pray you, give me time to answer that question.'

"Do you believe that speaking the truth is displeasing to God?"

"The voices have commanded me to tell certain things to the King, and not to you. Last night they told me many things for his welfare which I would that he knew."

"Could you not so deal with the voice as to make it carry that news to the King?"

"I know not whether the voice would do so. It could do so by God's will only. If God pleased, He himself could reveal it to the King, and I should be very glad."

"Why does the voice not speak to the King, as it did when you were in his presence?"

"I do not know whether it is God's will. Without the grace of God, I could do nothing."

A few more questions were put to her about her revelations. Then the examiner, recalling her words about "the grace of God," asked her, "Do you know if you are in a state of grace?" The question was a tremendous one—one that the wisest theologian might have hesitated to answer. He who was not in a state of grace was in a state of sin, an outcast from Divine love and favour. He, on the other hand, who dared declare himself in grace, was guilty of the deadly sin of pride. Even in that assembly many were shocked at the trap laid for Joan, and the monk Jean Fabri said plainly that she was not bound to answer. "You

would have done better to be silent!" exclaimed
Cauchon angrily, and the question was repeated,
"Do you know whether you are in the grace of
God?"

She answered, "If I am not, God guide me there; if
I am, God keep me there! If I knew myself to be
out of God's grace, I should be of all the world the
most sorrowful." Presently she added that she
believed the voices would not come to her if she were
in a state of sin.

The judges sat lost in wonder at her words. Her
simplicity had baulked their subtlety. There was a
long silence, and then Beaupère resumed the examination. He asked Joan about her village, her childish
life and work and pastimes. Thence he led her to
speak of the Ladies' Tree, the spring near it, and the
oak-wood of prophecy. Was the wood haunted? She
did not know; she had never heard. She knew that
sick people came to drink the water of the spring.
She had heard that the Ladies' Tree was haunted by
fairies; her godmother had told her so, but she herself
had never seen them. Her brother had told her that
many people at Domremy thought she had found her
inspiration under the Beautiful May; but that was
not true.

She spoke of the fairy legends so lightly and indif-
ferently as to frustrate beforehand any attempt
Beaupère might have made to connect them with her

revelations. He closed the day's examination by asking her whether she would not return to female dress. " Give me one," she said, "and I will wear it, if you will let me go home to my mother; otherwise, I will not have it. I will be content with this dress, since it pleases God that I shall wear it."

The tribunal sat again on Tuesday, February 27th. Before he began his questioning, Beaupère inquired how she had been in health since Saturday. "You can see for yourself; as well as I could be," answered the poor prisoner.

" Do you fast every day during Lent?" She resented those purely personal queries. " Does that concern your trial?" she asked. She was told that it did. " Yes, truly," she said; " I have always fasted this Lent."

Her voices were enquired about. She avowed that she had heard them since Saturday, that during her last examination they had been with her, that they had counselled her to answer boldly. She refused to speak without their counsel :—"For if I answered without leave, perhaps my voices would no longer be my warrant; but when I have God's leave, I do not fear to speak, for I shall have good warrant." She was examined about the nature of her voices, the appearance of her saints, their dress, their crowns. What saint had come to her first? She had seen St.

Michael first; not alone, but accompanied by the angels of heaven.

"Did you see St. Michael and the angels really and corporeally?"—"I saw them with my bodily eyes, as well as I see you ; and when they left me, I wept, and wished greatly they had taken me with them."

Being asked what St. Michael had said to her at his first coming, she refused to speak further of the saints, and referred the judges to the record of her examination at Poitiers. "I would that you could have a copy of those books," she said, "if it were God's will."

Beaupère spoke next of her dress, always a matter of offence to her enemies. It was a trifling thing, she said, the most trifling. So it then seemed to her, but it was soon to become a thing of terrible importance. She declared that she had put it on by command of God and the saints, not by advice of any man in the world. Being asked, "Do you think you did well to wear man's dress?" she replied, "I think everything I did by God's command was well done, and I expect good warrant and good help from Him."

"But in this special case, do you think you have done well to wear man's dress?"

"I have done nothing but by command of God."

The examiner reverted to her visions, and from them passed to the sword of St. Catherine. She was suspected of having used magic to make it fortunate, and he asked what charm she had put upon it. "None," she said; "I loved it because it had been found in the church of St. Catherine, whom I loved greatly."

" Did you never lay it on the altar that it might be lucky ?"—" Not that I remember."

" Did you never pray that it might be fortunate ?"— " Of course I wished my arms to be fortunate." The judge then asked her of her banner—did she love that best, or her sword ? " I love my banner forty times better than my sword," she replied.

Her campaigns were the next theme. She was questioned about the sieges of Orleans and Jargeau, and an assessor asked her if she had gone where the English were being killed ? " In God's name, indeed I have !" she said, marvelling doubtless at his simplicity. " How mildly you talk ! Why would they not leave France, and go back to their own country?" But she added that she herself had never killed anyone ; while charging the enemy, she had carried her banner, that she might not be tempted to use her sword.

When the tribunal next met (Thursday, March 1st), there was some discussion about the oath, and Joan, after taking it in her usual way, said, "In what concerns the trial, I will tell you the whole truth, as I would tell it were I before the Pope of Rome,"

Hereupon Beaupère inquired which Pope she acknowledged. "Are there two?" she asked. He did not
answer, but went on to speak of the Count of
Armagnac's letter. She admitted that the reply to it
had been written at her dictation, except certain
phrases, which she denied having used.

"Did you doubt which Pope the Count should
obey?" asked Beaupère.

"I did not know what to tell him, for he wished to
know which Pope God commanded him to obey. As
for myself, I hold and believe that we should obey
our lord the Pope who is at Rome."

She was asked about the cross heading some of
her letters ; did she always use that sign ? "Sometimes, not at others. I sometimes used to put *one*
cross as a sign to those of my party that they should
not do what I wrote."

Her first letter to the English was here read to her.
She acknowledged all of it except three expressions :
—*Render to the Maid*, ought, she said, to have been,
"render to the King," and she denied having dictated
chief of war, and *body for body*. She probably was
mistaken. The confident words that sounded extra-
vagant to her in her weakness and desolation must
have seemed natural enough in her day of hope.
But whatever words she might take back, she held
boldly to the sense of her letter. All of it that was
unfulfilled should yet come to pass. "Within seven

years," she said, "the English shall lose a greater pledge than before Orleans; and they shall lose all France."

"How do you know that?"

"I know it by revelation, and I am very grieved that it is delayed so long."

"When will it happen?"

"I know neither the day nor the hour."

"In what year?"

"You shall not know yet; but I would it were before St. John's Day."

Beaupère now cross-examined her concerning her saints. After many puerile questions, which to her who believed in the heavenliness of her visions must have sounded like blasphemy, he enquired about their speech. She told him their voices were good, beautiful, and gentle, and that they spoke in French. "Does not St. Margaret speak English?" he asked.

"How should she speak English, when she is not of the English party?"—a dangerous answer, which was remembered against Joan.

She was asked if she had conversed with St. Catherine and St. Margaret under the Fairy Tree. She did not remember. She never seemed able to understand those attempts to identify her heavenly friends with the unhallowed spirits of the wood. Had she talked with her saints near the spring?—Yes. What had they promised her?—"That does not concern

your trial," she said ; " but they told me that my lord
shall get back his kingdom whether his enemies will
it or no, and they have promised to lead me to
Paradise."

" Have you no other promise ?"

" That does not concern your trial ! . . . I do
not know when I shall be delivered, but those who
would put me out of the world may go before me.
. . . Speak to me of this in three months' time,
and I will answer you." In three months came to
her the great deliverance of death !

Being told she must give her answer then, as it
concerned the trial, she replied, " I have said you
shall not know everything. I must be rescued some
day. I want leave to speak; that is why I ask for
time."

" Do the voices forbid you to speak the truth ?"

" Would you have me tell what concerns the King
of France ? There are many things that have nothing
to do with the trial. . . . I know that my lord
shall have the kingdom of France. I know it as
surely as I know you are there before me, sitting in
judgment. I should die, but for this revelation that
comforts me daily."

Beaupère turned from Joan's consoling saints, to
ask her " what she had done with her mandrake ?"
The mandrake—the unclean and accursed plant of
witches ! She answered, " I have no mandrake, and

never had one. . . . I have heard there is one
near my village, but I have never seen it. I have
heard that it is an evil and dangerous thing to keep
one. . . . I do not know what it is good for." She
had no knowledge of those vile superstitions ; she
knew of no inspiration but that of the saints ; so her
examiners tried to degrade and vulgarise her lofty
visions. They asked in what shape St. Michael had
appeared to her. "I did not see that he had a
crown," she said, "and I know nothing of his
clothing."

"Was he naked ?"

"Do you think that God has not wherewithal to
clothe him ?"

"Had he hair ?"

"Why should it be cut off ?" she asked, impatiently.
Then, as if to reproach those priests and scholars
for their ignoble trifling, she said that she had
great joy in her saints' coming. "When I see them,
it seems to me that I cannot be in mortal sin. . . .
St. Catherine and St. Margaret hear me confess
sometimes."

"When you confess, do you believe you are in
mortal sin ?"

"I do not know whether I have been in it. I do
not think I have done its works. God grant I may
never have been in it ! God keep me from doing anything to burden my soul !"

The *sign* given to Charles formed the next subject of interrogation. She refused to reveal it, though she was assured that it concerned the trial. She said that of her own accord she had promised her saints not to reveal it, because unless she were bound by such a promise, she feared the secret might be extorted from her. She was asked whether, when she gave the sign, she had seen a crown on the King's head? "I cannot reply to that without perjuring myself," she said. Further questions were put to her about the crown—questions which probably developed the idea of it in her mind, and greatly affected her answers at a later examination.

Only forty-one assessors attended the sixth and last general session, which was held on Saturday, March 3rd. The examiner began with questions as to the aspect and reality of Joan's saints, and then passed on to the rescue they had foretold her. He asked, "Do you know by revelation that you shall escape?" "That does not concern your trial," she replied. "Would you have me speak against myself?"—an unwitting protest against the whole conduct of the proceedings.

Her dress, her banner and pennon, were next inquired about. Had not the Knights, her companions, their pennons made after the pattern of hers? Had she not told them that such pennons would be lucky? To this she answered, "I said to my men—'Go in boldly among the English!'—*and I went myself."*

"Did you not tell them to carry their pennons boldly, and they would have good luck?"—"I indeed told them what came to pass, and will come to pass again."

Had she not ordered pictures or images of herself to be made?—No, nor had she ever seen any image in her likeness. She had seen a picture of herself at Arras. She was represented kneeling on one knee, and presenting letters to the King.

Did she know that those of her party had caused masses and prayers to be said in her honour? "I know nothing of it," she answered, "and if they did so, it was not by my command. Nevertheless, if they prayed for me, I think they did no wrong."

"Do those of your party believe firmly that you are sent by God?"

"I do not know. I leave that to their consciences. But if they do not believe it, I am none the less sent by Him."

"Do you think them right in believing it?"

"If they believe that I am sent by God, they are not deceived."

"Did you understand the feelings of those who kissed your feet, your hands, and your garments?"

"Many were glad to see me. I let them kiss my hands as little as possible; but the poor people came

K

to me gladly, because I did them no unkindness, but helped them as much as I could."

"Did not the women touch their rings with the ring you wore?"—Many women touched my hands and my rings, but I do not know why they did so."

After some questions about children whom she had held at the font, about Friar Richard, and some minor details of the coronation, she was asked whether she had often received the sacraments during her journeys through the country? "Yes," she answered, and she confessed to having received them in man's dress, though without her arms. This was a plain avowal of sacrilege! A lesser offence of the sort was also proved against her. Had she not taken the palfrey of the Bishop of Senlis? She had bought the animal, and sent its price to the Bishop. She did not know whether he had received the money, but she had written to him, offering to return his palfrey. She did not care for it; it was useless for hard work.

She was questioned about the baby she had prayed for at Lagny. Did not people in the town say that she had prayed it back to life? "I never inquired about it," she replied.

Catherine of Rochelle, the siege of La Charité, and her imprisonment at Beaurevoir, were the next subjects brought forward. She was asked whether, after her attempt to escape by leaping from the tower, she had not cursed God in her anger. She answered, " It is not my habit to curse, and I have never blasphemed God nor the saints."

Here Cauchon informed the assembly that he had resolved not to call it for a time. Being loath needlessly to fatigue the assessors, he would finish the interrogations in private, before a few learned doctors, chosen to collect and write down the most important answers of the accused. Their report would afterwards be submitted to the assessors, whom he begged to reflect in the meantime on what they had already heard, and to communicate their ideas to himself, if necessary. Finally, he forbade them to leave Rouen without his permission before the end of the trial.

CHAPTER VIII.

THE EXAMINATIONS IN THE PRISON.

THE Bishop had several reasons for his new arrangement. Many of the assessors had been absent from the last two meetings of the tribunal. Some, doubtless, were fatigued by the long sessions, of which poor Joan also wearied greatly. Once she begged for a copy of the reports, so that in case she were re-examined in Paris, she could say, " Here are the questions put to me at Rouen, and my answers," and thus avoid a harassing repetition. The confusion of the proceedings greatly increased the strain upon her mind. Not only did the examiner flit from subject to subject—unskilfully, as it seemed, but really with intent to puzzle and bewilder her ; the assessors also were allowed to take up his questions, and put questions of their own, interrupting each other in such disorderly fashion, that Joan was often driven to say, "Good sirs, I pray you, speak one at a time !"

But others of those assessors must have withdrawn, because they were too just to sit calmly watching a great injustice, and too timid to protest against it. And a few such men also must have stayed, to be objects of fear and distrust to the Bishop. If they were permitted to watch the prisoner day by day, and hear her brave good words, who could tell how they might be infected by her boldness, and be moved to spoil his "fine trial" with their interference? Already, some had dared for one venturesome moment to come between him and his victim. She had wrung words of praise even from her enemies. "You say well, Joan!" cried some, when she baffled the examiner by a specially acute answer. "She is indeed a good woman! If only she were English!" exclaimed an English lord, one of those who had come to see the discomfiture of the Witch.

During the examination, there came to Rouen a noted lawyer, Jean Lohier, whose good opinion of the trial Cauchon wished to secure. Lohier studied the reports and other documents relating to it, and then, to Cauchon's rage and dismay, declared the whole affair illegal. The trial, he said, was not conducted after the usual forms; it was carried on in "a close and guarded place, where the assistants were not at full and perfect liberty to speak their full and free will;" it concerned the honour of the King of France, yet neither was he called, nor anyone to answer for him; lastly, the accused, a young and simple girl, had no counsel to advise her how to answer learned masters and doctors. Cauchon, having heard all this, went to his most congenial allies. "Here is Lohier meddling with our trial," he complained; "he wants to slander it, and calls it worthless. If we believe him, we must begin all over again, and what we have done will be good for nothing. By St. John, we will do no such thing! We will go on as we have begun."

Next day Manchon met Lohier in church, and inquired of him what he thought of the trial and of the prisoner. "You see how they are proceeding," answered the lawyer. "If they can, they will entrap her by her words—that is, by assertions where she says, *I know for certain*, touching her revelations; but if, instead, she were to say, *It seems to me*, I believe no man could condemn her. It appears that they are acting more through hatred than for any other cause; therefore I will stay here no longer, for I will have nothing more to do with it."

From the 4th to the 10th of March, Cauchon's most trusted colleagues were busy arranging materials for the second interrogation. This new inquiry, which occupied six days—Saturday, March 10th, Monday to Thursday, inclusive, and Saturday, March 17th— was held in Joan's prison-room, so that she no longer had even a slight change of place and air. Neither were her fetters taken off. Her limbs, so Massieu testified, were almost crippled by their galling weight.

The Bishop was generally present. The number

of assessors varied, but was always very limited. On March 11th, the vice-inquisitor received his chief's command to assist in the trial, and on the 13th he took his official place, attended by the monk Isambard de la Pierre. The task of questioning the accused was committed to Jean de la Fontaine.

The second examination is, to a great extent, a repetition of the first. It turns on the same subjects, and we see in it the same vices, only magnified, the same cruel unfairness, the same desire to falsify the reports, the same efforts to mislead and frighten the prisoner. The examiner shifted from point to point, seeking by the inconsequence of his questions to make Joan contradict herself. But that she never did. Her words, with one notable exception, were the words of plain and direct truth.

That one exception was her account of the "sign" given to Charles. The judges themselves had put into her mind the idea of a mysterious crown, brought to him by an angel, and out of it she evolved a tale or allegory with which mingled some recollections of the coronation. Thus she led the inquiry away from the secret there was between herself and her King—a secret which she was bound to keep faithfully, for nothing would have injured his cause more than any disclosure of the doubts he had felt about his own legitimacy. But true-hearted people cannot tell lies skilfully, even for a good end. The story was dragged

from her sentence by sentence, and the pain she told
it with is very visible.

At the first day's inquiry, she was asked, " What is
the sign that your King had to make him believe
you were sent by God?"

" It is beautiful and honourable," she replied; " it
is very good and worthy of belief, and the richest in
the world."

" Why would you not tell it?   You required a sign
from Catherine of Rochelle."

She answered that if Catherine's sign had, like
hers, been shown to many churchmen and nobles,
she would not have asked to see it.

" Does the sign still remain?" asked Cauchon.

" Indeed it does.   It will last a thousand years,
and more.   . . .   It is in the King's treasury."

" Is it gold, silver, precious stones, or a crown?"

" I will tell you no more about it. One could
imagine nothing so rich as that sign! The sign *you*
need is, that God shall deliver me out of your hands;
it is the surest He can send you."

The inquiry was renewed at the third day's examination. She made an effort to avoid it. " Would you
have me perjure myself?" she asked.

" Did you promise St. Catherine not to tell that
sign?"

" I have sworn and promised not to tell it, and
I have done so of my own will, because I was too

much beset to tell it. . . . I vow that I will speak of it no more to anyone."

But she had got into a tangle of falsehood, too easily proved false, too likely to serve her enemies' purpose, for them to let her escape out of it. She was compelled to go on as she had begun.

The angel, she said, when he brought the crown to the King, assured him that he should have all France, by God's help and the Maid's labour. " The crown was given to the Archbishop in the King's presence. . . . The Archbishop took it and gave it to the King. I was there. . . . It was brought into the King's room at the castle of Chinon. . . . I do not remember the day nor hour ; it was two years ago, after Easter. . . . The crown was of fine gold, so rich that I could not count its richness. . . . It signified that the King should have the kingdom of France. . . . The angel who brought it came from above ; he came by God's command. . . . He entered by the door of the room, and saluted the King, bowing before him, and reminding him of the patience he had shown in his great tribulation. . . . I came with the angel, and went up the steps to the King's room. . . . I said to the King, ' My lord, here is your sign, take it.' The angel returned by the way he had come."

She was asked where the angel had appeared to her.

" I was nearly always praying that God would send

the sign to the King. I was at my lodging in a good woman's house near the castle of Chinon when he came, and we went together to the King. . . . There were with him other angels that everyone could not see. . . . Some of them had wings, others had crowns. . . . St. Catherine and St. Margaret were of the company. . . . The angel left me in the little chapel, and I was very sad, and wept, and would willingly have had my soul go with him."

" Was it for your merit that God sent His angel?"

" He came for a great cause. It was that the King might believe the sign, and send help to the people of Orleans."

"And why by you rather than another?"

" It pleased God to drive out the King's enemies by means of a simple maid."

" Do you know whence the angel had that crown?"

" It was sent from God, and no goldsmith in the world could have made it so rich and beautiful. As to whence the angel got it, I leave that to God."

She was again and again examined about her revelations. Her voices, she said, had come to her first when she was thirteen years old. She had never spoken of them to her priest, nor to any other churchman, only to Robert de Baudricourt and her King. She had vowed her virginity to St. Catherine and St. Margaret.

Notwithstanding that vow, had she not tried to make a young man marry her against his will? In answer to this, she told the real story of her appearance before the court at Toul, where, she said, her voices had promised her she should gain her cause.

Had not the voices called her *daughter of God, daughter of the Church, daughter of a great heart?* She answered that before she had raised the siege of Orleans, and ever since, the voices had called her "Joan the Maid, Daughter of God." In great matters, she said, her voices had always guided her, and she took that for a sign that they were good spirits.

" Had you no other sign that they were good spirits?"

She replied that St. Michael had told her so; she knew him by his speech. The first time she saw him, she was afraid, and did not know who he was; but she soon learned to know him, and he taught her many things, and told her of the sorrow there was in the kingdom of France.

" In what form and kind, stature and clothing, did St. Michael appear to you?"

" He was in the form of a very true, brave man."

" Do St. Catherine and St. Margaret hate the English?"

" They love what our Lord loves, and hate what He hates."

" Does God hate the English?"

"Of God's love or hatred for the English I know nothing; but I know well that they shall be driven out of France, all except those that shall die there."

"Was God for the English when they prospered in France?"

"I do not know whether God hated the French, but I believe He would let them be beaten because of their sins."

She was asked why, when going to war, she had looked at her ring, engraved with the words, *Jesus-Maria*. It had been given to her by her parents.

"For pleasure," she said, "and for honour of my father and mother, and because, having that ring on my finger, I touched St. Catherine. She said that she had touched and kissed St. Catherine and St. Margaret. She had never offered garlands to those saints who appeared to her, but she had put flowers before their images in churches.

"When you hung garlands on the tree, did you do it in honour of your saints?"

"No."

"When those saints came to you, did you do them reverence by kneeling and bowing?"

"Yes, I did them all the honour I could, for I know those are indeed they who are in the kingdom of Paradise."

But had not those saints deceived her? Was it not at their command she had led that last sortie from Compiègne ? She answered that it was not so. In that, her voices had not guided her. But they had told her she must be taken before St. John's Day. "And I entreated them that when I should be taken, I might die soon, without long pain in prison. But they always bade me take everything patiently, and did not tell me the hour. If I had known it, I should not have gone ; and I often begged to know the hour, but they never told it."

" If the voices had ordered you to make the sortie, telling you that you would be taken, would you have gone ?"

" If I had known the hour, I should not have gone willingly. Yet I should have done their bidding, whatever might have befallen me."

Yet had she not disobeyed those voices ? Was it not against their command that she had tried to escape from Beaurevoir ? She owned that in so doing she had sinned, but her saints had seen her necessity, and known how she was tempted, and they had saved her life. She had confessed her sin, and God had forgiven her.

" Did you do great penance for it ?"

" I bore a great part of my penance in the hurt I had from falling."

" Was it a mortal sin ?"

" In what concerns that, I trust to our Lord."

She was questioned about her frustrated escape

from Beaulieu. Had God given her any leave to escape from prison?

"I have often asked for it," she said, "but I have not had it yet."

"Would you go now if you found the opportunity?"

"If I saw the door open, I would go, because that would be God's leave for me. . . . It is said, *Help thyself, and God will help thee.* I tell you this, that if I do go, you may not say I went without leave."

The Bishop being absent from the fourth day's examination, Fontaine inquired what Joan had meant by the warning she had once given him. She answered—

"I said to my lord of Beauvais—'You say you are my judge; I know not if you are, but take heed that you do not judge amiss, for you are putting yourself in great danger.'"

"What is that danger?"

"St. Catherine has told me I shall have help. I know not whether it will be release from prison, or whether at my trial some disturbance may happen by which I shall be rescued. I think it must be one or the other. What my voices tell me oftenest, is that I shall be delivered with a great victory; and then they say—'Fret not thyself because of thy martyrdom. Thou shalt come at last to the kingdom of Paradise.'"

This was no conscious prophecy of her death. By her martyrdom she understood the bitterness of her prison; it was martyrdom enough! And yet she added—"I know not if I shall have more to bear, but I trust in God."

"If your voices have told you that you shall come at last to Paradise, are you assured that you will be saved, and not damned in hell?"

"I believe firmly what my voices have told me, that I shall be saved, as firmly as if I were already *there.*"

Her happy trust in God, and ignorance of dogma, had led her into the church-invented sin of over-presumption.

"That reply is of great weight," said the inquisitor.

"And I hold it for a great treasure," she replied.

"After that revelation, do you believe that you cannot do mortal sin?"

"I do not know. I trust God in all." She said that she hoped to be saved if she kept her vow, and guarded her virginity, both of body and soul.

"Do you think you have need to confess, since you believe the promise of your voices that you will be saved?"

"We cannot keep our conscience too clean," was her wise answer.

She wished greatly to attend mass, but the favour was denied her, because of her dress. She was asked

whether she would rather wear a woman's dress and
hear mass, or keep on her man's dress and not
hear it.

" Certify me," she said, " that I shall hear mass if I
wear woman's dress, and I will answer you."

" I do certify it," said the judge.

" I will answer you. Let me have a gown made
long, down to the ground, and give it to me, that I
may go to mass ; then when I come back I will again
put on the dress I wear now."   She entreated to be
allowed to hear mass " in that good town, for the
honour of God and our Lady," but her judges refused,
unless she would promise, " simply and absolutely," to
keep on woman's dress.   They would give her none
except a short peasant costume, such as she had
formerly worn—thinking, perhaps, to degrade her
thus to her old peasant estate, and declare her an
impostor.

" Give me," she pleaded, " a dress like that of a
citizen's daughter, a long gown and a woman's hood,
and I will put it on to go to mass."   But she would
not promise to wear it afterwards.   Dear though the
services of the Church were to her, her honour was
dearer.   The man's dress that had been her protection
in the camp was her defence in the dungeon, and her
unwillingness to lay it by reveals what dangers that
dungeon held for her.   Her judges, with amazing
dulness, or more amazing wickedness, could not or

would not understand her motives. She shrank from explaining. Shortly again they offered her a change of dress, and she again refused it, but she said, "If I should be brought to death, and if I must be unclothed for my death, I entreat the lords of the Church to grant me a woman's shift, and a kerchief on my head."

"You have said that you wear man's dress by command of God ; why do you ask for a woman's shift in case of your death ?"

" Only let it be long," was all her answer.

Later on, she was reminded of what she had said, that she would wear a woman's dress if allowed to leave her prison.

" If I were let go in a woman's dress," she replied, " I would soon put on man's dress, and do what my Lord has commanded me. On no account would I take an oath not to arm myself, and wear man's dress, to do our Lord's pleasure."

She was asked about the angels on her banner. " Had you them painted in the likeness of those that appear to you ?"

" I had them painted as they are represented in churches."

" Did you ever see them as you had them painted ?"

" I will tell you nothing more."

" Why had you not the light that comes to you painted also ?"

L

"It was not commanded."

"Did you ask your voices whether, if you carried your banner, you would win all the battles you engaged in ?"

"They told me to carry the banner boldly, and God would help me."

"Did you help the banner most, or the banner you ?"

"Whether the banner was victorious, or I, it was all through God."

"But was the hope of victory founded on your banner or on you ?"

"It was founded on God, and on none other."

"Did you not wave your banner over the King's head when he was crowned at Reims ?"

"Not that I remember."

"Why was it carried to the coronation rather than those of the other captains ?"

"It had been at the work ; good reason that it should be at the honour."

De la Fontaine began the fifth day's business by " charitably exhorting " Joan to defer to the judgment of the Church. In return, she demanded to have her answers seen and examined by the clergy, that she might be told if there were anything in them against the Christian faith. She would then consult her *counsel*, and if she had said anything contrary to the Christian faith, she would not uphold it. The judge explained to her the difference between the Church triumphant and the Church militant, and required her to submit all her words and actions to the decision of the latter.

She refused to answer further then, and at the next examination the question was repeated—"Will you leave to the judgment of the Church all your words and deeds, both good and evil?"

She answered—"As for the Church, I love it, and would uphold it with all my power, for the sake of our Christian faith. It is not *I* who should be kept from going to church and hearing mass! As for my coming, and the good works I have done, I refer them to the King of Heaven, who sent me to Charles, son of Charles, King of France, who *shall* be King of France."

"Will you submit your deeds to the judgment of the Church?" insisted the examiner.

"I submit them to God who sent me, to our Lady, and to all the blessed saints in Paradise. It seems to me that our Lord and the Church are one, and that no difficulty should be made. Why do you make a difficulty, and say they are not one?"

De la Fontaine set himself to explain to her that important article of the Catholic faith, *Unam Sanctam Ecclesiam*—"There is the Church triumphant, which is God, the saints, the angels, and the souls that are saved; and there is the Church militant, which is our holy father the Pope, the cardinals, the prelates, the clergy, and all good Christians and Catholics—which Church collectively cannot err, and is governed by the Holy Spirit. Will you not submit to this Church militant?"

"I came to the King of France from God, the Virgin Mary, and all the blessed saints of Paradise, and the victorious Church above; and to that Church I submit all my good works, and all I have done or shall do! As regards the Church militant, I will answer no more now."

That afternoon, she was asked whether she would consider herself bound to satisfy the Pope more fully than she had satisfied the Bishop of Beauvais.

"Take me before him," she replied, "and I will answer all I ought to answer."

Here the monk Isambard de la Pierre spoke— "Appeal to the Council of Basle," he said to her. She asked what that council was, and he explained that it was an assembly of the Catholic Church, where were present as many of her own as of the English party.

"Oh!" she cried, "since there be some of our party there, I will submit to the Council of Basle!"

The Bishop heard her with great anger. "Hold your peace, in the devil's name!" he shouted;

and he prevented the scribe from recording her appeal.

"Ah," said she, "you write what is against me, but what is for me you do not write."

Those appeals and disputes were not to Cauchon's liking, and the examination was shortly brought to a close.

CHAPTER IX.

THE ARTICLES OF ACCUSATION.

DURING the ensuing week, the vice-inquisitor and a few chosen assessors met twice at Cauchon's lodging to arrange the next proceedings. They decided to reduce Joan's answers to certain formal articles, which might conveniently be submitted to the court, or might serve, if necessary, as the basis of a fresh inquiry. It being thought advisable first to let Joan hear the reports of her examination, they were read to her in prison, and she found in them little to object to.

On Monday, March 25th, the Bishop again assembled his colleagues, and read to them the completed articles. They were approved, and it was agreed that Joan should hear them, and be required to answer them, due time being given for her replies. If she delayed too long, or refused to answer any article, she was to be declared contumacious and excommunicate, and to be held convicted of the offence imputed to her in it. The charge of defend-

ing and urging the accusations was given to Jean
d'Estivet.

Next day, Joan was brought into the room adjoining the castle hall, where were present thirty-eight
assessors. Jean d'Estivet having sworn that he was
acting neither for favour, nor revenge, nor fear, nor
hatred, Cauchon advised the accused that she was
before doctors and churchmen learned in human and
divine law, who desired to treat her with all clemency,
not wishing to chastise her body, but only to lead
her into the path of truth and salvation. And he
recommended her, because of her ignorance in letters
and other matters, to choose for counsel one or many
of those present, or to receive an adviser of his
choosing. He also demanded from her an oath that
she would speak the truth.

She answered:—" Firstly, for your admonition
touching my welfare and our faith, I thank you
and all the company. For the counsel you offer me
I thank you also, but I have no intention to depart
from the counsel of our Lord. As for the oath you
would have me take, I am ready to tell the truth
about all that concerns your trial." She took that
oath, and Thomas de Courcelles began reading the
articles. The reading, with Joan's replies and the
comments of her judges, occupied two days.

The preamble was a key to what followed. It
described the Maid as a sorceress, a false prophetess,

an invoker of demons, a practiser of magic arts. It
called her superstitious, schismatic, sacrilegious, idola-
trous, an apostate, a blasphemer of God and the
saints, scandalous and seditious, disturbing and pre-
venting peace, inciting to war and bloodshed, shameless and immodest, abominable to God and man, a
law-breaker, a seducer of princes and people, a
usurper of the honours due to God, and a suspected
heretic.

There were seventy articles, and in every one of
them some incident of her life or some answer she
had given her judges was shamefully distorted and
falsified. She heard them quietly, showing only by
her sad gravity and frequent silence the scorn she
must have felt for the scholarly perverters of truth
who had drawn them up. She occasionally referred
back to her former examinations. Some of the
articles she answered, others she either absolutely
refused to answer, or promised to consider if time
were granted her.

She was accused of having from her early youth
practised magic, and made compacts with evil spirits
(Art. 2). She had received no religious training, but
had been taught witchcraft by old women, and
frequented places haunted by fairies (4, 5). Here
she answered, "As for fairies, I know not what they
are, but I learned my belief well and duly, as a good
child ought to do."

She had hung on the Ladies' Tree garlands which vanished during the night (6). She had worn the mandrake in her bosom, hoping to get good luck by it (7). She had gone to Neufchâteau against her parents' will, and taken service there at an inn frequented by soldiers and light women. It was there that she had learned to ride and use arms (8). At that time she cited before the court at Toul a young man who once had promised to marry her, but afterwards refused to keep his word, because of the ill company she kept (9). She had boasted to Robert de Baudricourt that, after the fulfilment of her mission, she would have three sons, of whom the eldest should be Pope, the second Emperor, and the third a King (11). To this she simply replied that she had never said such a thing at all.

She had not only worn man's dress, saying it was by God's will, and thus impiously making God contradict His own written law, but her dress had been of such wanton fashion and costliness as to offend all honest men (13). And she had held to man's attire, choosing rather to abstain from hearing mass than to put it off (16). Here the judge reproached her with not only dressing, but behaving like a man, and forsaking women's work. "As for women's work," she replied, "there are plenty of women to do it."

She had bewitched her ring, her banner, and the

pennons she and her people carried (20). She had dared to write letters full of things hurtful to the faith, and to head them with a cross and the names Jesus and Mary, and send them to the Regent and the English before Orleans (21). She had used the words Jesus-Maria and the cross as a signal to her party not to obey her letters (24). She had boasted of knowing futurity, which knowledge belongs only to God (33). She says she has seen the saints corporeally, and avers that they speak not English, but only French, thus shaming them by supposing that they hate a good Catholic nation (42). She has on various occasions been guilty of blasphemy (46, 47). She believes that her apparitions are saints and angels, and yet she gives no good reason for her belief, nor has she consulted any churchman on this matter (48). She has worshipped those spirits, has kissed the ground over which, as she says, they have passed, and has done them reverence, thus exposing herself to suspicion of idolatry and compact with demons (49). She invokes them and consults them daily (50).

Joan defended her saints. " To believe in them, I need no counsel of bishop or priest. . . . I will call them to my help as long as I live."

" How do you call them ?"

" I beseech our Lord and the Virgin to send me counsel and comfort."

" In what words do you beseech them ?"

She answered :—"'Very gentle God, in honour of Thy holy passion, I entreat Thee, if Thou love me, to reveal to me how I shall answer those churchmen. I know well the command by which I have worn this dress, but I know not in what manner I should leave it off. Therefore, be pleased to teach me !' And soon they come," she added.

She was accused of having lived among men, of having made herself a chief of war, and employed men about her person instead of women (53, 54).

" If I was chief of war," she said, " it was to beat the English. My government was of men, but in my lodging I had usually a woman with me, and in the field I lay down armed and clothed."

Being charged with her refusal to tell the whole truth at her examination (Art. 60), she replied, " I would not reveal the King's counsel, because it does not concern the trial. As for the sign given to the King, I told it because the churchmen *condemned* me to tell it."

The remaining articles accused her of pride, of presumption, of blasphemy, sedition, heresy, and persistence in error, and, lastly (Art. 70), declared that the truth of all the afore-named charges had been recognised not only by the people at large, but by Joan herself in presence of upright and credible witnesses. To the accusation of blasphemy and heresy she replied, " I am a good Christian ; that I call God to witness." She was asked finally whether, if she *had* sinned against the Christian faith, she would submit herself and her faults to the Church. " On Saturday afternoon," she said, " I will answer."

On Saturday, which was Easter-even, the Bishop, the vice-inquisitor, and a few assessors went to her prison, and again put the question, which had now become of vital import to her :—Would she submit to the Church ? She replied that she would, unless it required of her what was impossible. It would be impossible for her to take back anything she had said or done by command of God, or to cease doing His will. Not even at the Church's bidding would she in anything disobey God.

" If the Church militant tells you that your revelations are false, or diabolical, or superstitious, or things of evil, will you submit them to its judgment ?"

"I will submit them to God, whose command I will do always. I know well that what is contained in my trial came to me by His command, and it would be impossible for me to do the contrary of what I have affirmed was done by His command."

" And if the Church commanded you to do the contrary ?"

"I would submit to no one but our Lord, and would always do His good bidding."

" Do you believe that you are subject to the Church

on earth—namely, our holy father the Pope, the cardinals, archbishops, bishops, and other prelates of the Church?"

"Yes, our Lord being served first."

"Have you commandment from your voices not to submit to the judgment of the Church militant?"

"I do not answer out of my own head. What I answer is by command of my voices, and they do not forbid me to obey the Church—*our Lord being served first.*"

She had answered enough, and Cauchon and his creatures left her. Easter Monday and the two days following they devoted to revising the seventy articles and Joan's replies, and condensing them into twelve articles, which became the real basis of the trial. Those new articles were drawn up with infinite skill, so as to impose on anyone who had not followed Joan's examination. They were written with apparent fairness; their style is grave and judicial; they are, on the surface, a calm statement of very damaging facts. But in them facts are distorted and words perverted from their true sense. Joan's saints become evil counsellors, who meet her by the Fairy Tree, and incite her to disobedience and immodesty. Her belief in the saints becomes contempt for Christ. Her revelations are sorcery. Her dress is a proof of lightness and irreverence. The cross on her letters is sacrilegious. Her courage is unwomanly cruelty.

Her mission is unfilial disobedience and presumption.
Her attempted escape from Beaurevoir is an attempt
at suicide. Her trust in the saints is wicked pride ;
her belief in their love for her party, blasphemy and
lack of charity ; her reverence for them is idolatry ;
her loyalty to their counsel is rebellion against the
Church. Copies of the Twelve Articles were sent
to all whose opinion was desired or needed, and with
each copy was sent a letter from the Bishop, requesting a speedy reply, and by its terms almost dictating
what that reply was to be.

Most of the answers were against Joan. A meeting
of doctors, held at Rouen on April 12th, pronounced
that her revelations were lies or sorcery—her acts
scandalous and impious—her words rash and presumptuous—her whole conduct schismatic, blasphem-
ous, unfilial—her notions savouring of heresy. Many
of those who were consulted by letter agreed exactly
with this opinion ; others refused to decide until they
knew the decision of the University of Paris ; a very
few suggested that nothing should be settled without
an appeal to the Pope or the general council.   .

Meanwhile, Joan fell sick. Her close captivity, the
weary anguish of her days, the pining she had for
some religious service at the Easter season—all her
sorrows of mind and body told upon her at last, and
she lay so ill and fever-stricken, that it seemed as if
pitying death must deliver her from the cruelty of

men. The English were greatly disquieted at her sickness. Warwick sent her two physicians, charging them to try and cure her, "for," said he, "the King has paid dearly for her; he would not for the world have her die, except by justice." D'Estivet took them to her dungeon. They asked the cause of her illness, and she told them she had eaten of a carp sent her by the Bishop of Beauvais, and that had made her ill. She doubtless suspected poison, not understanding how precious her life was to her enemies. D'Estivet upbraided her furiously, calling her vile names, and he so excited her and increased her fever, that Warwick sent him word to let her alone for the future.

The physicians bled her, and the fever passed away, leaving her very feeble. Cauchon visited her· in her weakness, taking with him several churchmen, and proceeded to "charitably exhort" her, offering to let some learned doctor instruct her in matters of faith. He told her that if she still resisted, she would expose herself to abandonment and great peril, from which he would affectionately preserve her. She thanked him, and replied—"Seeing what sickness I have, it seems to me that I am in great peril of death; and if such be God's will towards me, I pray you to grant me confession, and our Saviour, and burial in holy ground."

"If you would have the sacraments of the Church,"

said Cauchon, "you must do as good Catholics should, and submit to the Church."

" I cannot now answer you about that otherwise than I have answered."

" The more you fear for your life, the more you should amend it ;" and he urged her to submit to the Church.

" If my body die in prison," she repeated, " I trust you will have it laid in hallowed ground ; but if you do not so, I trust in God."

The Bishop still pressed obedience on her, and the doctors who were with him also entreated her— " Submit to the Church, and we will give you the Sacrament !" She thought herself dying, and the temptation was a strong one, but she held bravely to her convictions. " I will not answer otherwise than before ! I love God, I serve Him, I am a good Christian, and I would serve and uphold the Church with all my might. . . . I would have the Church and all good Catholics pray for me."

Her youth and wonderful strength conquered her sickness, and on May 2nd she was able to appear before the whole body of assessors. She had not heard the Twelve Articles, and it was needful that she should hear them; but the astute Bishop deceived both her and the court. She knew nothing of the articles, and as a modified version of them was read to her, she took them for a new sort of exhortation ;

while those assessors who were not in Cauchon's secret, seeing how quietly she listened, thought she had already heard and agreed to them in their complete form."

She was again questioned about the Church. " I believe in the Church on earth," she said; "I believe it cannot err; but as for my words and deeds, I submit them to God, who has caused me to do all I have done."

" Do you believe that you have no judge on earth ? Is not our holy father the Pope your judge ?"

Here she might have done prudently to appeal again to the Pope, but her brain, weakened by sickness, worn by wearisome questioning, did not work quickly. Yet a sublime answer was ready. " I have a good Master, our Lord, to whom, and to none other, I trust in all."

" If you will not believe the Church, and the article *Ecclesiam Sanctam*, you will be a heretic, and must be punished by fire."

" I will not answer otherwise ; and if I saw the fire, I would say to you what I have said, and nothing else."

The judge insisted on knowing whether she would submit to the Pope.

" Take me to him," she said, " and I will answer him."

The examination was further prolonged, but she

M

would give no satisfactory answers, and at last ended it perforce by keeping a resolute silence.

In those days there was a way of compelling prisoners to speak, to which the judges of this young prisoner had not yet resorted. But now they resolved to try it. On May 11th, she was led from her cell to the torture-chamber, where she found the Bishop and a few of his colleagues. Cauchon told her that she was suspected of having kept back much of the truth, and that she must reveal it at once, or be put to the torture; and he showed her the ghastly instruments about the room, and the executioners ready for their dreadful work.

She answered, " Though you should tear me limb from limb, and send the soul out of my body, I would tell you nothing more. And if I did speak differently, I would afterwards tell you that you had *compelled* me to speak."

She was so bold, that the Bishop asked her whether the saints had been with her. Yes, she said, on the day following her last examination St. Gabriel had come to her. She had asked her voices whether she should submit implicitly to the Church, and they had told her that if she desired help from God, she must trust Him in all. She was asked, had she inquired of her voices whether she would be burnt ? She had done so ; " and they have told me," she said, " to trust in God, who will help me."

Steadfast in soul, feeble in body as she was, she would probably have died under torture, and have died silent. So her judges would not risk it then, but three days later they consulted whether to use it. Most of them opposed it as being unnecessary; among the minority in its favour were Thomas de Courcelles and Nicolas Loyseleur.

The chapter of Rouen, which had delayed giving its opinion on the Twelve Articles, met on May 4th, and agreed to the general finding against Joan. Some days later arrived the decision of the University of Paris, and on the 19th, Cauchon imparted it to the assessors, whom he had convened for the purpose. He also read to them two letters from the University: one to the King of England, thanking him for his devotion to the Church, and advising him to bring Joan's trial to a speedy conclusion; the other to himself, praising him for his zealous conduct of the affair, and commending the doctors who had taken part in it.

The University, after pronouncing against Joan on each one of the articles, declared that, if she was in her right senses when she made the affirmations stated in them, she was :—schismatic, in forsaking her obedience to the Church; false to the faith, in contradicting the article *Unam Sanctam Ecclesiam;* apostate, in having cut off her hair and forsaken woman's dress for that of a man; vicious and a

sorceress, in saying she was sent by God, without
proving her mission by miracles or Scripture testimony; astray from the faith, being under the *anathema*
of the Church for choosing not to communicate rather
than leave off man's dress ; deceived, in saying she
was as sure of going to Paradise as if she were already
there.

Most of the assessors agreed with those opinions of
the Paris doctors, and advised that Joan should once
more be warned of her danger, and, in case she
remained obstinate, should be given over to the
secular power. A minority were in favour of sen-
tencing her at once, without any warning.

On May 23rd, she was brought before the Bishop,
who had with him two other prelates and seven
of the assessors. One of these, Pierre Maurice, was
charged to exhort her, which he did by addressing to
her the substance of the Twelve Articles, following
each with the comments pronounced on it by the
University. This done, he gave her a wordy admonition, condemning her revelations, and counselling her
to submit to the Church. " But if you do not so," he
concluded, " know that your soul shall be damned,
and I fear the destruction of your body, from which
things may Christ preserve you !"

She still was firm. " I will hold to what I have
said and maintained at the trial. If I were at the
judgment, and saw the fire kindled, and the faggots

alight, and the executioner ready to feed the fire, and if I were *in* the fire, I would not say otherwise ; but I would maintain what I said at the trial, even to death."

Here Cauchon asked the promoter and the prisoner whether they had anything more to say. Both answered that they had not, and he, having declared the trial ended, called upon Joan to appear on the morrow and hear her sentence.

CHAPTER X.

TO the English soldiery, who were clamorous for Joan's execution, her mere death would have seemed enough. They wanted only to be rid of her, and of the fear of her that had chilled their courage. They wanted to carry on their conquests and their plunderings, secure from the hindrances which, so they believed, she could send them even from the deepest dungeon.

But the English statesmen and their willing servants wanted more. If they allowed her to die a martyr's death, would she not after her death be as dangerous to their cause as ever she had been in life? Would not the cause of Charles seem truer and dearer than ever to his people if one of God's saints perished in maintaining it? Would not loyalty to him, love for France, hatred to the usurper, appear a sacred legacy left by the Maid, to be cherished in every French heart? To prevent those things, Joan must be proved false to her saints, and

to the cause she had defended. The noble words she
had spoken before a few, she must be made to take
back before a great multitude, who would spread far
and wide the story of her inconstancy.

Early on May 23rd, Jean Beauperè went to her
prison, and told her she was to appear and be preached
to in public, and either receive sentence of death, or
avert it by a promise to obey the Church. He was
followed by her false counsellor, Loyseleur, who tried
to threaten or cajole her into submission. " If you
will do what I tell you," he said, " you shall be saved,
and much good shall befall you, and you shall have
no harm, but shall be restored to the Church."

She was taken to the cemetery of the abbey of St.
Ouen, where two scaffolds had been built. One was
occupied by Cauchon, the Cardinal of Winchester,
and a crowd of scholars, priests, and nobles. The
other, facing it, was reserved for Joan and her
attendants, and for Guillaume Erard, who had been
appointed to preach the sermon.

He took for his text, " The branch cannot bear
fruit of itself except it abide in the vine," and
expounded how the Church was the vine in which all
true Catholics must abide. Joan had separated
herself from the Church by her iniquities. She was
a witch, a heretic, a blasphemer !—there were no words
too strong for the priest to fling at her. She listened
calmly, until his unwise ardour led him to revile her

King. "O France," he cried, "thou art greatly deceived! Thou hast always been a very Christian land, and now Charles, who calls himself thy king and governor, has trusted, like a heretic and schismatic, which indeed he is, to the words and deeds of a worthless and infamous woman, full of all dishonour. And not he only, but all the clergy in his obedience and lordship, by whom she was examined, as she says, and not rebuked." Here he turned and pointed to Joan :—"It is to thee, Joan, that I speak, and I tell thee thy King is schismatic and a heretic!"

"By my faith, sir," she answered, "in all reverence, I dare say and swear to you, on peril of my life, that he is the noblest of all Christians, and the one who best loves the faith and the Church."

"Make her hold her peace!" cried the preacher, angrily. Then he went on with his sermon, at the conclusion of which he again addressed Joan :— "Here are my lords your judges, who frequently have called and required you to submit your words and deeds to our holy mother the Church, showing that in both were many things which, as it appears to churchmen, were good neither to say nor to hold."

"I will answer you," she said. "As for submission to the Church, I *have* answered them. I have told them to send a report of all I have said and done to Rome, to our holy father the Pope, to whom, *and to*

God first, I appeal. As for my words and actions, I have said and done them by God."

Presently she spoke further in defence of her King. "I charge my words and deeds on no one, neither on my King, nor on any other. If there be any fault in them, it is mine only."

Being asked whether she would revoke those words and deeds which had been reproved, she repeated her appeal to the Pope. She was told that the Pope was too far off, that each bishop was judge in his own diocese, and that she must submit to the Church as there represented. Erard showed her a form of recantation, and summoned her to abjure. She was unlearned in words, and she asked what did that word *abjure* mean. Massieu was ordered to explain it to her, and he did so, at the same time advising her to be cautious, and warning her in how great danger she would be, if, after renouncing the things mentioned in the schedule, she dared to return to them.

When he had done speaking, she said in a firm voice—"I appeal to the universal Church whether I ought to abjure them or no!" Erard was furious, for he had counted on persuading her by his eloquence. "You shall abjure them instantly, or be burnt this very day!" he exclaimed.

Loyseleur, who had kept by her side, now importuned her: "Do as I told you—accept woman's dress." "Do as you are counselled," cried others;

"why will you die ?" The very judges entreated her : "Joan, we pity you so much ! You must take back what you have said, or we must give you up to secular justice." She still protested that she had done well ; that she believed in the faith and in God's commandments ; that she appealed to the Pope. The tumult of beseeching and threatening voices was in her ears. "You take great pains to seduce me !" she said, looking round upon the eager monks.

Now, above the confusion of sounds, rose the Bishop's voice reading the sentence of death. From the scaffold where Joan stood, she could see the grim figure of the executioner, waiting for her below, and the English soldiers, impatient that he should have her. The Bishop read on. The churchmen about her pleaded and promised. At last the desolate, bewildered girl gave way. She said, "I will submit to the Church."

No time was given her to change her mind or make reservations. Massieu read to her the form of abjuration, which lasted "about as long as a Paternoster," and took up six or eight lines of writing, and she repeated it after him, smiling as she did so, like a child repeating some strange lesson.

Then Calot, a secretary of Henry VI., laid a paper before her and bade her sign it. Still smiling, she traced a round o. "I cannot read nor write," she said, so Calot took her hand and guided it to sign her name, *Jehanne.* An evil trick had been played her. In her ignorance she had been made to sign, not the short and simple formula read to her by Massieu, but a long list of the crimes imputed to her, and a confession of them. It is this substituted document that appears among the records of the trial.

The Bishop now turned to Cardinal Beaufort, and asked him what should be done next. " Admit her to penance," was the reply, and he read the form of sentence he had ready in case of an abjuration. Having enumerated Joan's offences, and pronounced her guilty, he declared her restored to the Church, and freed from excommunication. *But*, as she had sinned against God and the Church, he condemned her to perpetual imprisonment, with " the bread of affliction and the water of anguish," that she might learn to repent of her crimes, and commit them no more.

She had been promised deliverance from prison, and here was decreed her a lifetime of captivity. She had been tricked and deceived, and while she stood dumb with the shock and the pain, Loyseleur, who had lied to her, came sidling up to congratulate her on having "done a good day's work." Then she found her voice. There was a sort of comfort for her yet ; she had submitted to the Church, and the Church, even while punishing her, was bound to protect her. " Now you men of the Church," she said, " take me to your prison, and leave me no longer in the hands of the English." No one answered her, but the Bishop turned to the guards and bade them "take her back to the place whence she had been brought."

Even had he wished to grant her prayer, he could hardly have ventured to do so then. For the English were wild with rage when they saw her saved, as they thought, from death. They had interrupted the proceedings with angry murmurs, and had even thrown stones at the judges. The Cardinal's chaplain told Cauchon to his face that he was a traitor to King Henry, but Winchester understood the Bishop's tactics, and bade his chaplain be silent. Warwick, who was more obtuse, complained that the King was ill served, and that Joan would escape. "Do not fear, my lord," said one of the doctors who overheard him; "we shall soon have her again!"

That afternoon, the Bishop, the vice-inquisitor, and several doctors visited Joan, and having pointed out to her how mercifully she had been treated, they exhorted her to offend no more, warning her that if she did so, the Church would utterly cast her off. They next desired her to take off her male attire and put on the woman's clothes provided for her, and this they forced her to do in their presence. Then they left her, deceived, humbled, borne down by regrets and bitter self-reproach.

The next two days Joan spent in tears and

remorse, in listening to the taunts and fighting off the insults of her vile jailors. She was left utterly at their mercy. Some priests tried to see her, but they were driven back with threats and blows by the men-at-arms about the castle.

When she awoke on Sunday morning, she asked her guards to unchain her that she might rise from her bed, to which she was fettered by her ankles. They undid the chain, and one of them came and took away her woman's dress, throwing her in its stead the clothes she had laid aside. "Sirs," she said, "you know this is forbidden me ; I cannot wear it," and she implored them to have pity on her, and give her back the clothes she had promised to wear.

She pleaded with them until noon, but in vain, and at last she was forced to rise and put on the dress they had given her.

Then went out the news that she had relapsed. Several churchmen came and again tried to see her, but the soldiers refused to admit them, and menaced them with their swords, calling them Armagnacs and false traitors. Next day, however, the Bishop, the vice-inquisitor, and some assessors got access to the prisoner. Manchon was with them, and afterwards he bore witness how they found her:—"Forlorn, weeping, bruised, and disfigured, so that he had pity on her."

The assessor Marguerie ventured to inquire how a woman so strongly guarded had been able to obtain the forbidden dress, but he was roughly told to be silent. The Bishop asked Joan why she had put it on. She answered, according to the official report, that she had done so of her own accord, and because she liked it best.

"But you promised and swore not to return to it."

"I never meant to take oath that I would not wear it again. . . . It is more seemly to wear man's dress, I being among men." She said that she had a right to wear it, because the judges had not kept their promise to free her from her chains, and let her go to mass and receive the sacrament.

They reminded her of her abjuration. "I would rather die," she cried, "than live in chains! But if you will let me go to mass, and will take off my chains, and put me in a peaceful prison where I may have some woman with me, I will be good, and obey the Church."

Cauchon took no notice of her appeal, but inquired whether she had heard her voices since Thursday. She answered, Yes.

"And what have they told you?"

"God has sent me word by St. Catherine and St. Margaret what great pity it is that I was guilty of the treason of abjuring to save my life, and that I have *damned* myself to save my life." In three authentic

MSS., the words *responsio mortifera* (fatal answer) are written on the margin over against this bold reply.

She confessed that the saints had foretold her abjuration. On the Thursday they had bidden her answer the preacher boldly—the bad preacher, who had accused her of things she had never done. She was asked whether she still believed in her mission. She answered—"If I were to say that God did not send me, I should condemn myself. It is true that God sent me. . . . My voices have told me that I sinned greatly in confessing that I had not done well. It was through fear of the fire that I said what I did."

"Do you believe that your voices are St. Catherine and St. Margaret ?"

"Yes, and they are from God."

"But on the scaffold you said that you had lied in boasting that they were St. Catherine and St. Margaret."

"I did not mean to say or do so. . . . I never meant to deny my revelations, and if I said so, it was falsely, and through fear of the fire. . . . I would rather do my penance at once, and die, than suffer any longer in this prison. . . . I have never done anything against God or the faith, whatever you may have made me revoke. . . . I did not understand what was in the schedule of abjuration." She again promised to wear woman's dress if she were put into a safe prison.

But her fate was settled now. The Inquisition had no pardon for one who relapsed. The judges left her, a few daring to be sorry for the brave creature, but most of them openly and indecently glad. In the courtyard they found a number of English waiting for news, among them the Earl of Warwick. " Farewell, farewell !" cried the Bishop, as he passed him ; "be of good cheer—it is done !"

Next morning he called the assessors to a last conference. Several of their number had left Rouen immediately after Joan's recantation, either supposing the trial to be over, or foreknowing and fearing to witness its real issue. To those that remained, Cauchon recapitulated the events of the past week— the admonition by Pierre Maurice, Joan's abjuration, and her relapse. Then, having caused the report of her last examination to be read, he demanded the opinion of all present. They all agreed that she had relapsed, and not one voice was raised to excuse her, or to inquire what had driven her to disobedience. Her guilt was proved ; let her be given over to the secular power ; but first—so counselled most of the assessors—let her once again hear the formula of abjuration, and be charitably exhorted for her soul's welfare, and warned that she had nothing more to hope for in this world.

The Bishop thanked the assembly, and ordered a citation to be drawn up, summoning Joan to appear next morning in the Old Market-Place of Rouen, there to receive her final sentence. She did not hear her doom that night, but early in the morning (May 30th), the monks Martin Ladvenu and Jean Toutmouillé were sent to make it known to her and prepare her for it.

When Joan returned to her male attire and abjured her abjuration, she knew well enough what she was risking. " I spoke through fear of the fire," she said to her judges. Still, to her strong youth and her high courage, death may have appeared vague and far off, as it generally does appear to youth and courage. Besides, had not her voices promised her a great deliverance ? Perhaps God would send His angel. Perhaps her king would send an army, and she would hear, first the French cannon outside Rouen walls, and then the French war-cry in its streets, and her own people would come and take her out of prison, that she might lead them again to victory. She must often have dreamed such dreams, but there was an end of them now.

The grave faces and grave words of the monks showed her the dreadful reality, close and vivid, and for a little while youth and womanhood and human weakness had their way with her. She wept piteously and tore her hair in the wildness of her

N

anguish. " Alas," she cried, " will they treat me so
horribly and cruelly ?   Must my body, that never
was defiled, be consumed to-day and turned to ashes ?
Ah ! I would sooner seven times be beheaded than
be burnt !   Alas, if I had been in the prison of the
Church, to which I submitted, and if I had been
guarded by churchmen and not by my enemies, it
would not have befallen me thus miserably !   Oh, I
appeal to God, the great Judge, against the wrong
and injustice done to me !"

While she was thus lamenting, Cauchon came in,
with Pierre Maurice, Loyseleur, and two or three
others.   Seeing him, she cried, " Bishop, I die by
you !"

" Ah, Joan," he answered, "be patient.   You die
because you have not kept the promise you gave us,
and because you have returned to your former
iniquities."

" Alas," she said, " if you had put me in a prison of
the Church, and given me right and proper keepers,
this would not have happened.   Therefore I appeal
against you before God."

The Bishop had come to try and make her retract
again, but she was firm now, and he and his companions went away shortly, leaving her alone with
Martin Ladvenu.   Maurice looked kindly at her as he
went, and she said to him, " Master Pierre, where shall
I be to-night ?"

" Have you not a good hope in God ?" he asked.

"Ah yes, and by God's grace, I shall be in Paradise."

After confessing and receiving absolution, she desired to have the Eucharist. Massieu had come to serve the citation, and the monk sent him to ask Cauchon whether he might administer it. Cauchon conferred a little with his companions, and then bade the usher "go and tell Brother Martin to give her the Eucharist, and whatever she may ask for."

She received the sacrament with tears, and with deep penitence and devotion. Thenceforth her faith was unshaken, and she failed no more.

At nine o'clock she left the prison, clothed now in a woman's long gown, and wearing a mitre, inscribed with the words, *Heretic, Relapsed, Apostate, Idolatress.* A cart was waiting for her, and she got into it, accompanied by Brother Martin and the usher Massieu. A guard of about eight hundred soldiers surrounded her to keep off the crowd, but suddenly there rushed through their ranks a haggard and miserable figure. It was Nicolas Loyseleur, who, seized by late and vain remorse, had come to ask forgiveness of her whom he had betrayed. But before he could reach her, the soldiers drove him back, and Joan probably neither saw nor heard him, for she was weeping and praying, her head bowed upon her hands.

When she looked up, she saw beyond the soldiers a dense throng of people, most of them grieving for her, many of them lamenting that this thing should be done in their city. " O Rouen, Rouen," she cried, " is it here that I must die ? "

At last she reached the Old Market-Place, a very large space, where had been raised three scaffolds : one for the Bishop of Beauvais and his colleagues, and for all the prelates and nobles who desired to see the show ; another for Joan and some priests and officials ; the third, also for Joan—a pile of stone and plaster, raised high above the heads of the crowd, and heaped with faggots. In front of it was a tablet bearing this inscription :—

Joan, who has called herself The Maid—liar, pernicious, deceiver of the people, sorceress, superstitious, blasphemer of God, presumptuous, disbeliever of the faith of Christ, boaster, idolatress, dissolute, invoker of devils, apostate, schismatic, heretic.

Master Nicolas Midi, a famous doctor from Paris, preached Joan's last sermon, on the text, " If one member suffer, all the members suffer with it." At its close, he addressed her :—" Joan, go in peace ! The Church can no longer defend you ; it gives you up to the secular power."

Then the Bishop spoke to her. He did not read the form of abjuration, as had been advised, for she would have boldly disavowed it, and would so have spoilt a scheme he had concocted. But he admonished her to think of her salvation, to remember her misdeeds, and repent of them, and to obey the counsel of her confessor. Finally, after the usual inquisitorial form, he declared her cut off from the Church, and delivered over to secular justice.

She needed no exhortation to prayer and penitence. For a while she seemed to forget the gazing crowd and the cruel judges. She knelt and prayed fervently —prayed aloud with such passionate pathos, that all who heard her were moved to tears. Even Cauchon wept. Even the Cardinal was touched. She forgave her enemies; she remembered the King, who had forgotten her; she asked pardon of all, imploring all to pray for her, and especially entreating the priests to say a mass for her soul. Presently she asked for a cross. An English soldier broke a stick in two and made a rough cross, which he gave her. She kissed it and put it in her bosom, but she begged Isambard de la Pierre, who was by her, to bring her the crucifix from a church near at hand. It was brought, and she embraced it, weeping, calling upon God and the saints.

But the men-at-arms were growing impatient. "Come, you priests," shouted one of them, "are you going to make us dine here?" The bailiff of Rouen, as representing the secular power, should now have pronounced sentence of death, but he seemed afraid of delaying the soldiers, two of whom came up and seized Joan. "Take her! take her!" he said, hurriedly, and he bade the executioner "do his duty." The Bishop's *fine trial* had, after all, an illegal and informal ending.

The soldiers dragged Joan to the pile, and as she climbed it, some of her judges left their platform and rushed away, fearing to behold what they had helped to bring about. She was fastened to the stake, high up, that the flames might gain slowly upon her, and that the executioner might not be able to reach her and mercifully shorten her agony. "Ah, Rouen!" she cried again, as she looked over the city, bright in the May sunshine—"Ah, Rouen, Rouen! I fear thou wilt have to suffer for my death!"

The executioner set fire to the pile. The confessor was by Joan's side, praying with her, comforting her so earnestly, that he took no notice of the ascending flames. It was she who saw them and bade him leave her. "But hold up the cross," she said, "that I may see it." Now Cauchon went to the foot of the pile, hoping perhaps that his victim might say some word of recantation. Perceiving him there, she cried aloud, "Bishop, I die by you!"

And now the flames reached her, and she shrank from them in terror, calling for water—holy water! But as they rose and rose and wrapped her round, she seemed to draw strength from their awful contact.

She still spoke. Brother Martin, standing in the heat and glare of the fire, holding the cross aloft for her comfort, heard her dying words :—"*Jesus ! Jesus ! Mary ! My voices ! My voices !*" Did she hear them, those voices that had said, " Fret not thyself because of thy martyrdom ; thou shalt come at last to the kingdom of Paradise"?—" Yes," she said, "my voices *were* from God ! My voices have not deceived me !" Then, uttering one great cry—"*Jesus !*" she drooped her head upon her breast, and died."

.   .   .   .

The common folk soon added their tale of signs and wonders to the simple and terrible truth. An English soldier, who greatly hated the Maid, had sworn to bring a faggot to her burning, and he threw it on the pile just as she gave that last cry. Suddenly he fell senseless to the earth, and when he recovered, he told how at that moment he had looked up, and had seen a white dove fly heavenward out of the fire. Others declared that they had seen the word *Jesus*— her dying word—written in the flames. The executioner rushed to a confessor, crying that he feared to be damned, for he had burned a holy woman. But her heart would not burn, he told the priest ; the rest of her body he had found consumed to ashes, but her heart was left whole and unharmed.

Many, not of the populace, were moved by her death to recognise what she had been in life. " I would that my soul were where I believe the soul of that woman is!" exclaimed Jean Alespée, one of the assessors. "We are all lost, we have burnt a saint!" cried Tressart, a secretary of the King of England. Winchester—determined that, though she might be called a saint, there should be no relics of her—had her ashes carefully collected and thrown into the Seine.

The tidings of her death went speedily through France. They found Charles in his southern retirement, and nowise disturbed the ease of mind and body that was more to him than honour. They reached Domremy, and broke the heart of Joan's stern, loving father. Isabelle Romée lived to see her child's memory righted and her prophecies fulfilled.

CHAPTER XI.

THE END OF THE WAR—THE TRIAL OF ATONEMENT.

FOR a week Cauchon and the rest kept quiet, thinking it wise, perhaps, to let the first indignation at Joan's martyrdom pass off before they attempted to maltreat her memory. At this time the anger and sorrow of the populace found lively expression, and not one of the judges could appear in the streets of Rouen without being pointed at and openly reviled as a murderer. Nor did this horror of them pass away. Long afterwards, the people told how those who were guiltiest of the Maid's death came to an evil end: how the Bishop of Beauvais died in a fit of apoplexy; how Nicholas Midi became a leper; how Jean d'Estivet's body was found lying in a gutter at the gates of Rouen, and how the infamous Loyseleur died suddenly at Basle.

On June 7th, the Bishop got up a document purporting to be the account of statements made by Joan on the morning of her execution. According to

this report, she *had* abjured a second time, and confessed that her voices had played her false, and that
she herself had deceived the people.   Manchon was
ordered to sign it, but he doubted its truth, and would
have nothing to do with it.   The good scribe was
very sorrowful for Joan's death and his own share in
her trial.   " He could not be comforted for a month,"
he afterwards told, " and therefore, out of the money
he had got by the trial, he bought a little missal, that
he might pray for her."   The document, unsigned as
it was, was added to the official records of the proceedings.

During the month of June the English Government
issued three letters, all meant to throw disgrace on
the Maid, and excuse or exalt those who had
destroyed her.   The first was addressed to the Pope,
the Emperor, and the kings and princes of Christendom.   The second was a letter of guarantee to all
concerned in the trial.   The third was a lengthy
manifesto to the prelates, nobles, and cities of France.
The University of Paris also wrote to the Pope, the
Emperor, and the College of Cardinals, giving an
account of the affair.

These letters were eagerly received and believed
by the friends of England and Burgundy, and
the cruellest calumnies were spread abroad to cast
dishonour upon the Maid.   In Paris, the Church took
an active part in that bad work.   A solemn procession

was organised (July 4th), and the chief inquisitor preached a sermon, giving a garbled account of Joan's life and death. From the age of fourteen (so he declared), she had worn man's dress, much against the will of her parents, who would gladly have killed her, but for their fear of doing a sin. She had left her home, accompanied by "the Enemy of Hell," and since then had been a slayer of Christian folk, full of wrath and bloodthirstiness. Having retracted her errors, she had been admitted to penance—namely, four years' imprisonment on bread and water; but instead of submitting, she had required to be served "like a lady" in her prison. Then the Enemy, who had some dread of losing her, appeared to her in the guise of St. Michael, St. Catherine, and St. Margaret, and said to her—"Evil creature, who out of fear hast left off thy man's dress, fear not, we will guard thee against everything!" Thereupon she at once returned to her former attire, which she had hidden in her bed. Being for this crime given up to secular justice, she called upon those "enemies" who had appeared to her in the form of saints; but they came not, and she repented when it was too late.

The English now carried on the war with fresh spirit, and at first gained some successes. In July, their brave adversary, Barbazan, was defeated and slain at Bulligneville, where he was fighting on the side of René of Anjou. In August, the French were beaten near Beauvais, and it was in this encounter that the shepherd-boy of Gevandun was made prisoner. Like Joan, he was taken within Cauchon's jurisdiction, and he too was claimed by the Bishop, and kept for a while in ecclesiastical prison. The poor impostor, a creature weak in mind and body alike, was, some months later, given up to the English. He figured, bound and tied upon a horse, in the procession which attended Henry's entry into Paris, and shortly afterwards, without trial or ceremony, was thrown into the Seine.

At the end of October, La Hire fell into the hands of the English, and the town of Louviers, which he had held for nearly two years, was forced to capitulate. But public feeling was turning steadily against the foreigner, and even the Parisians began to long for a French king. Bedford vainly tried to please them and gratify their love of change and pageant by having Henry VI. crowned at Notre Dame (December 16th, 1431). Though there was no real joy at his coming, the young king was greeted with the show of rejoicing. He was met at the gates of Paris by representatives of the city and the University. He passed under triumphal arches, and his progress was delayed by the performance of mysteries usual on such occasions.

As he rode by the palace of St. Pol, his grandmother, Isabeau, stood at a window and gazed out at him. Being told who she was, he saluted her, whereupon she turned away, weeping bitterly. The Queen had good cause for weeping. She was expiating by a most sorrowful old age her evil days of pride and power. The English, whom she had helped so greatly, treated her with neglect or scorn. The Parisians never spoke of her but with contempt, and those who went by her dwelling would point at it, saying aloud, " There lives the cause of all the sorrow that is in France !"

The coronation was an utter failure, both in itself and in its effect on the people. None of the great French nobles were present. The King was crowned, not by a French prelate, but by the Cardinal of Winchester, who, having supplied the expenses of the ceremony, chose to take a prominent part in it. Everything was done more according to English than to French custom, and all classes of the Parisians were offended during the subsequent festivities. The magistrates and doctors who attended the banquet were hustled by a crowd of common folk, who were suffered to push their way into the hall, and even to carry off the dishes from the tables. No prisoners were set at liberty ; no privileges were granted to the citizens. There was not even the customary largess : " We should have got more at a goldsmith's wedding !" cried the angry populace. Henry was soon taken back to Rouen, where he remained for a year before his final return to England.

In 1432 the English lost a friend, or rather a non-enemy, at the French Court, in the person of La Trémouille, whom some indignant nobles removed from it by force. Charles VII., who was now completely influenced by his beautiful mistress, Agnes Sorel, took the loss of his favourite very coolly. Agnes had been introduced to Charles by his mother-in-law, Queen Yolande, and his wife, the pious and patient Marie of Anjou, received her and treated her courteously. All three ladies were opposed to La Trémouille, and helped to ruin him. He was replaced by ministers of a very different sort, whose patriotic counsel taught the King a new and more worthy policy.

Towards the close of the year died Bedford's wife, Anne of Burgundy, who had done much to preserve the alliance between her husband and brother. In the following April, the Regent married Jacqueline of Luxembourg, a lively and beautiful girl of seventeen, whose father, the Count of St. Pol, was a vassal of Burgundy. The marriage took place without Philip's consent, or even his knowledge, and his anger at the insult to himself and his sister's memory was turned to good account by the friends of the King of France. The Cardinal of Winchester tried to reconcile the two dukes, but his efforts came to nothing.

Gradually and surely, all France was being won to the side of Charles. All classes longed for peace.

Philip himself desired it. The Pope, the Council of Basle, the princes of Christendom, were willing to aid in bringing it about. At last, in the summer of 1435, a great peace-conference was held at Arras. Philip went there in great pomp. The Pope was represented by his legate, Nicholas Albergati; the Council of Basle, by the Cardinal of Lusignan. Cardinal Beaufort, with a chosen company of nobles, prelates, and scholars, both French and English, defended English interests. Charles VII., Queen Yolande, the Dukes of Brittany, of Lorraine, of Alençon, the University of Paris, and nearly all the chief cities of France, sent their delegates. Learned doctors from nearly every country in Europe attended and took part in the proceedings.

All proposals made by the English deputies were rejected, and they in their turn refused to allow the great concessions demanded of them. The presiding cardinals sided openly with France, and devoted their energies to reconciling the King with the Duke of Burgundy. Seeing this, and not choosing to witness the complete discomfiture of his party, Beaufort withdrew from Arras, taking with him the whole English embassy.

While the conference was going on, John of Bedford died (September 14th), and exactly a week later, peace was signed between Charles and Philip. By this Treaty of Arras, Philip gained possession or

sovereignty of many towns and much territory, and
was exempted from doing homage during the life
of Charles VII. The King, by his ambassadors,
entreated pardon for the murder of John the Fearless
at Montereau, and the Duke, laying his hand upon
the cross, declared that he forgave Charles for that
crime, and promised never to remind him of it more.
Then the cardinal-legate absolved Philip and his
vassals from their oath of enmity against Charles,
and the nobles of France and Burgundy swore to
live thenceforward in friendship. In those days, such
vows were lightly made and easily forgotten. " I
have already sworn to five treaties during this war,"
exclaimed the Lord of Launay, when he took the
oath, "and not one of them has been kept. But I
promise before God that this one shall be kept by
me and by my followers, and never broken!"

On September 29th, Isabeau of Bavaria died—of
joy, so it was said, at hearing of the Peace of Arras.
She was buried at St. Denis, but with so little
ceremony, that the Parisians, always apt for discontent,
regarded her mean funeral as an insult to the ancient
royalty of France.

The capital had ever been ready to follow the Duke
of Burgundy's lead, and in a few months it opened its
gates to a Franco-Burgundian army (April, 1436),
which the people received with cries of " Peace !
peace ! Long live the King and the Duke of Bur-

gundy !" The small English garrison was suffered to depart unmolested, except by the derisive shouts of the populace. So was fulfilled one of Joan's prophecies —"Within seven years the English shall lose a greater pledge than before Orleans."

Charles did not take personal possession of Paris until late in the following year, when he made his solemn entry, and was most joyfully welcomed, the citizens shouting "Noël!" before him, and weeping for gladness. They expected his very presence to cure all the ills that had so long been afflicting them. But he remained with them only a little while. Paris was to him a city of hateful memories. The country beyond the Loire, his home by necessity in his time of trouble, was his home by choice in the days of his prosperity, and there he continued to hold his court, only occasionally visiting the northern provinces.

The winter after his departure was a dreadful one for all the Isle-of-France, and especially for the capital. Bands of English soldiers, and of those freebooters called *Ecorcheurs* (Skinners), plundered the surrounding country. Famine and the plague took possession of the city. The inhabitants died by thousands. Hundreds of houses were left deserted, and were torn down for firewood. Wolves entered the place by the river, and prowled about the ruined and desolate streets.

o

The war dragged on without any decisive event.
Charles VII., who at last had overcome the indolence
that had caused Joan so much sorrow, took an active
part in it. The English captains, and especially
Talbot, the most daring of them all, maintained their
country's honour against great odds. In 1444, a
truce for two years was signed, chiefly through the
influence of the Duke of Orleans, who had been
released in 1440 on payment of a heavy ransom.
England was growing very weary of the strife. At
the head of the peace-party there was the Cardinal
of Winchester, an aged man now, worn-out and
disappointed; he was eagerly opposed by the Duke
of Gloucester, who, perhaps, was loath to see the loss
of those conquests for which his two brothers had
lived and died.

In 1445, Henry VI. married Margaret of Anjou, a
kinswoman of Charles VII., and there was hope in
England that a lasting peace would come of the
union. But the hope was a vain one. Henry,
instead of receiving a dowry with his bride, had
promised to give the sovereignty of Maine and
Anjou to her father René, nominal Duke of those
provinces. The cession was delayed, and Charles,
who, as René's suzerain, claimed a right to interfere,
sent an army to occupy Maine (1448). In the
following year he invaded Normandy, where town
after town either received him without resistance,

or became an easy conquest. Guienne, left unaided by the English government, fell yet more easily into his power; and before the close of 1453, Calais alone remained to England of all that she had possessed in France, or had won there during the Hundred Years' War.

. . . .

For long after her death, Joan seemed almost forgotten, except by the common people, who fondly cherished her memory, and told marvellous stories of her exploits. But in the spring of 1436 she was recalled to all men's minds by a rumour that she was not dead; that, somehow—by a miracle—by connivance of her judges—she had escaped from the fire, and, after being hidden for years, had shown herself in the neighbourhood of her own village.

The woman who dared to personate her, a worthless adventuress named Claude, appeared soon at Metz, where many people of repute, and even Joan's brother, recognised her as the veritable Maid of Orleans. She was rather like Joan. She rode gracefully, and was skilful in the use of arms. She answered several questions so well that her identity seemed proved to many whose eagerness to believe in it kept them from being over-inquisitive. In November she married a knight of good family, Robert des Armoises, to whom she bore two sons. Three years later she visited Orleans, where she was acknowledged, though with no great enthusiasm, and presented with gifts of wine and money.

She ventured to appear before Charles, whom she recognised among his nobles, much as the real Joan had done. He was not deceived by her, but he greeted her courteously, saying, "Maid, my friend, welcome back, in the name of God, who knows what secret there is between us!" Hearing those words, she was struck with a terror that betrayed her, and was forced to confess her imposture.

But as many would still have it that she was indeed the Maid, the Parliament and the University of Paris sent for her, and had her brought thither much against her will. She was condemned to stand on the "marble table" in the court-yard of the palace, and there publicly relate the whole story of her life, which had been anything but reputable. She owned but one good quality, an adventurous courage, which had carried her through several campaigns. She had been with the Pope's army; she had fought the English in Poitou, and had served under Marshal de Retz. After her exposure, she was let go, as being too contemptible for further punishment.

In 1450, the year following the recovery of Normandy, Charles, whom time and the influence of good advisers had changed greatly for the better, determined that she to whom he owed his kingdom should at last be vindicated before the whole world. He

gave to Guillaume Bouillé, a doctor of Paris and a
royal councillor, letters patent authorising him to
collect information concerning Joan's trial, and bring
it before the council. Bouillé examined seven persons,
Martin Ladvenu, Isambard de la Pierre, Toutmouillé,
Beaupère, Guillaume Duval, who had been one of the
assessors, Manchon, and Massieu. Charles, however
improved as a king, remained a cold and selfish man,
or the details given by those witnesses would have gone
near to breaking his heart. As it was, he must have
felt keen remorse when he heard the story of that
long agony which he had done nothing to prevent or
to interrupt.

In 1452 the affair was put into the hands of the
Pope, in the person of his legate, Cardinal d'Estoute-
ville, Archbishop of Rouen, who opened a court of
inquiry in that city. Being obliged to return to
Rome, the cardinal empowered Philip de la Rose,
treasurer of the cathedral, to carry on the proceedings.

But here policy came in, and seemed as though it
would stop them altogether. Joan's trial had been
conducted by authority of the King of England, and
it was a delicate matter for the King of France to
overthrow a verdict which his brother-sovereign had
found good and acted upon. However, Charles, or
some adviser of his, conceived the idea of altering the
revision from an affair of state into a mere private
business. Joan's relations were brought forward; her

mother and her brothers appealed to the Pope for justice to her memory.

The documents of the trial were sent to Rome, and read carefully by learned doctors, who, after comparing the Twelve Articles with the reports of the examinations, pronounced the former to be illegal and unworthy of credit. In June, 1455, Calixtus III., lately elected Pope, granted the petition of the Du Lis family, and commissioned the Archbishop of Reims and the Bishops of Paris and Coutances, aided by an inquisitor, to inquire into the trial of Joan of Arc.

On November 7th, the three prelates and the inquisitor, Jean Bréhal, met in the cathedral of Notre Dame in Paris, where Joan's aged mother came before them, supported by her sons, and followed by a great procession of nobles, scholars, and honourable ladies. She presented the petition she had made to the Pope, and the letter whereby he granted it, and the commissioners took her aside, heard her testimony, and promised to do her justice. Ten days later she again appeared before them, and her petition and the Pope's answer were read publicly. Then her advocate, Pierre Maugier, explained that the petitioners denounced three persons only of those concerned in the trial—the chief judge, Pierre Cauchon, the vice-inquisitor, Jean Lemâitre, and the promoter, Jean d'Estivet. Those men were all dead, but their heirs or representatives were cited to appear at Rouen and answer the charges brought against them. On December 20th an advocate came forward, and in the name of Cauchon's family declined to defend his conduct or oppose the inquiry.

On February 17th the judges heard read a hundred and one articles, enumerating the grievances of the petitioners, and forming an abstract of the faults and illegalities of the trial. The case was then adjourned, that Joan's history might be further investigated.

And now the dead heroine was confronted with her dead judges, to their shame and her enduring honour. Messengers were sent into her country to hear the story of her innocent childhood and pure, unselfish youth. Through her whole life went the inquiry, gathering testimony from people of all ranks. The peasants whom she had loved and tended in her early girlhood, the priests who had heard her in confession, the men who had fought by her side, the women who had known and honoured her, the officers of the trial, and many who had watched her sufferings and beheld her death—all were called to speak for her now. They testified to her goodness, her purity, her single-hearted love for France, her piety, her boldness in war, and her good sense in counsel. All were for her—not one voice was raised against her. Rouen, the place of her martyrdom, became the place of her triumph.

All that mass of evidence, and the documents relating to both trials, having been scrupulously examined, Jean Bréhal was charged to draw up a summary of the conclusions. These were :—That Joan's visions came from God ; that the purity of her motives, and the good she did to her country, justified her in leaving her parents and wearing man's dress ; that she had in very fact been a submissive daughter of the Church. The late Bishop of Beauvais was declared a partial, and therefore an incompetent judge ; and the vice-inquisitor, the assessors, and all Joan's advisers and exhorters, were censured as having hindered or perverted justice.

On July 7th, the Commissioners met in the hall of the Archbishop's palace to give sentence. Jean du Lis was present, and Isabelle Romée and her other son were represented by proxies, but no one appeared to dispute the justice of their demands. After enumerating the motives for their decision, the judges declared the Twelve Articles false and calumnious, and condemned them to be torn from the records and publicly destroyed ; they pronounced the whole trial and both judgments to be polluted by wrong and calumny, and therefore null and void ; finally, they proclaimed that neither Joan nor any of her kindred had incurred any blot of infamy, and freed them from every shadow of disgrace.

By order of the tribunal, this new verdict was read

publicly in all the cities of France, and first at Rouen, both in the cemetery, the scene of Joan's abjuration, and in the Old Market-Place, where she had been cruelly burnt. This was done with great solemnity; processions were made, sermons were preached, and on the site of her martyrdom a stone cross was soon raised to her memory.

In her honour, the people of Orleans instituted an annual religious festival, which, with occasional interruptions, has been kept up to the present day. The city also took care of Isabelle du Lis until her death, which happened two years after the vindication of Joan's memory; and the Duke of Orleans gave a grant of land to her brothers, in recognition of her services.

The world has no relic of Joan. Her armour, her banner, the picture of herself that she saw at Arras, have all disappeared. We possess but the record of a fair face framed in plentiful dark hair, of a strong and graceful shape, of a sweet woman's voice. And it seems—and yet, indeed, hardly is—a wonder that no worthy poem has been made in her honour. She is one of the few for whom poet and romancer can do little; for as there is nothing in her life that needs either to be hidden or adorned, we see her best in the clear and searching light of history.

APPENDIX I.

THE FAMILY OF JOAN OF ARC.

By letters patent, granted in December, 1429, Charles VII. conferred nobility and the privileges thereunto appertaining upon Joan of Arc, her relations, and all their descendants born in wedlock, not only in the male, but also in the female line. The females of her family had, furthermore, the right to ennoble their husbands, should those be of inferior rank. This unusual privilege was, however, withdrawn in 1614.

Joan did not avail herself of the honours given to reward her services, but her brothers adopted the armorial bearings granted them, and took the name of Du Lis. The eldest of them, Jacques, or Jacquemin, who had remained quietly at Domremy, died before the second trial. The King bestowed pensions on Pierre and Jean du Lis, and the latter was made bailiff of Vermandois, and, later on, captain of Vaucouleurs. Joan's mother lived in Orleans from the year 1440 until her death in 1458, and was supported by a pension paid to her by the city.

The Du Lis family became extinct in the male line in the 18th century; but several French families of good position claim to be descended in the female line from Jacques and Isabelle d'Arc.

APPENDIX II.

THE SCHISM IN THE CHURCH.

THE three Popes, respecting whom the Count of Armagnac wrote to consult Joan, were Martin V., elected by the Council of Constance, and the anti-Popes, called Clement

VII. and Benedict XIV., who had both been irregularly elected in Aragon, after the death of Benedict XIII. in 1424. The answer attributed to Joan is as follows :—

"JESUS + MARIA.

" Count of Armagnac, my very dear and good friend, Joan the Maid lets you know that your letter has reached me, the which tells me that you have sent it hither, to know of me which of the three Popes therein mentioned you ought to believe. Of which thing I at present cannot well inform you for certain, until I shall be at Paris, or elsewhere in quiet, for at present I am too much prevented by the war. But when you shall know that I am in Paris, send a message to me, and I will tell you truly and with all my power whom you should believe, and what I shall know by the counsel of my true and sovereign Lord, the King of all the world, and what you ought to do. I commend you to God. God keep you.

" Written at Compiègne, the 22nd day of August, 1429."

APPENDIX III.

THE FALSE JOAN.

AMONG the accounts of the city of Orleans are found the following entries relative to Claude des Armoises :—

" To Pierre Barantin, for paying Fleur-de-Lis [a herald or messenger], on Thursday, the 9th of August, for having brought letters to the town from Joan the Maid, 48 sous."

" To Jean du Lis, brother of Joan the Maid, on Wednesday, the 21st of August, 1436, a gift of 12 livres, for that the said brother of the Maid came before the town-council to ask for money that he might go back to his sister."

" To Regnault Brune, on the 25th day of the same month, for having given drink to a messenger who had brought letters from Joan the Maid, 2 sous 8 deniers."

"To Cœur de Lis [another messenger], on the 18th day of October, 1436, for a journey taken by him, on behalf of the said town, to the Maid, who was at Arlon, in the Duchy of Luxembourg ; and for carrying letters from the said Maid to the King, at Loches, 6 livres."

"The 11th day of September, for bread used at the arrival of the said Cœur de Lis, who brought the afore-named letters from Joan the Maid, and for furnishing drink to the said Cœur de Lis, who said that his thirst was very great, 2 sous 4 deniers."

"On July 19th, 1439, for ten pints of wine given to the said Dame Joan, 14 sous."

"On July 30th, for meat bought to give to Madame Joan des Armoises, 40 sous ; for 21 pints of wine for dinner and supper, given to the said Joan, 28 sous."

"August 1st, for ten pints of wine given to her at dinner, when she left the town, 14 sous."

On the 4th of September, the Lady des Armoises returned to Orleans, as we see by an entry for wine supplied on that day to her and her attendants. The citizens presented her with 210 livres, "for the benefits done by her to the town during the siege ;" and in natural consequence of their recognition of her, the annual mass celebrated for Joan of Arc was discontinued.

APPENDIX IV.

JOAN OF ARC IN LITERATURE.

It is from the reports of her two trials that we gain most of our information respecting the Maid. The chroniclers of her time, even when favourable to her, generally give us but scant details of her life. Seeing in her but one among many actors in the war drama—and an actor too that was soon removed from the scene—they fail to recognise that the sorrowful time following her capture was also the time of her most true glory. The chief chroniclers of her century that mention her are—The *Bourgeois de Paris*, a clerk of the University, a gossiping and delightful writer, but a bigoted Burgundian ; Enguerrand de Monstrelet, also a Burgundian, and much prejudiced against the Maid ; Thomas Basin, author of a history (in Latin) òf Charles VII. and Louis XI.; Perceval de Cagny, a devoted retainer of the House of Alençon, and, as such, most favourable to Joan; Jean Chartier, a clerk of St. Denis, whom Charles VII. appointed chronicler to the Kings of France ; Jacques de Bouvier, called Berri, a herald, whose chronicle extends from the year 1402 to the death of Charles VII.; the author of the *Chronique de la Pucelle*, attributed by Vallet de Viriville to Guillaume Cousinot, a nephew of the chancellor of the Duke of Orleans; Pierre Cochon, writer of the *Chronique Normande*, who was at Rouen during Joan's trial; Philip of Bergamo, who published in 1479 his *De claris electisque mulieribus*, a work wherein legend almost eclipses history; Pope Pius II. (Æneas Sylvius Piccolomini) mentions Joan in the 6th book of his memoirs.

In 1576 was published by the city of Orleans the *Histoire et Discours du Siége*, an account of its deliverance, compiled probably from the registers kept during the siege. In the same century, Etienne Pasquier, in his *Recherches sur la France*, renders justice to the Maid's virtue and heroism. Charles du Lis, a descendant of her brother Pierre, published, in 1628, a collection of inscriptions, &c., composed in her honour.

During the 18th century, historians began to study the reports of Joan's trials, but it is in our own time that her life has received full attention. This is in great part due to the important publication of M. Jules Quicherat, comprising the full reports of both trials, the documents relating to the Maid, and extracts in prose and verse from contemporary chroniclers and others. The chief modern historians of Joan are—Lenglet-Dufresnoy ; L'Averdy ; Lebrun des Charmettes ; Villiaumé, a descendant of the Du Lis family ; Sismondi (in his *Histoire de Français*); De Barante (in his *Histoire de Ducs de Bourgogne*);

Michelet, and Henri Martin (in their Histories of France);
Vallet de Viriville (*Hist. de Charles VII.*); Henri Wallon,
whose most excellent work obtained the "Prix Gobert"
from the Académie Française.

Among the innumerable poets who have written of the
Maid of Orleans, the earliest was the scholarly Christine
de Pisan, an aged woman at the time of Joan's triumph,
which she celebrated in very laudatory though somewhat
prosaic verses. Martin le Franc, a Burgundian, and
Martial d'Auvergne, author of the *Vigiles de Charles VII.*,
a rhymed chronicle, did justice to the Maid in their
works; and François Villon kept her memory green in his
famous ballad of *Les Dames du Temps Jadis.* The
poets of the 16th and 17th centuries made a heroine of
her, but a heroine after their fashion, stilted and artificial.
Their absurdity culminated in the *Pucelle* of Chapelain, a
dull and long-winded arrangement of platitude and
allegory.

Concerning the detestable *Pucelle* of Voltaire, it is
enough to quote Southey's words, "I have never been
guilty of reading it." Southey's own fine poem on the Maid
fails entirely to render a just idea of her character,
though it is disfigured by none of those sins against fact
and good taste which deface Schiller's otherwise beautiful
tragedy, *Die Jungfrau von Orleans.*

INDEX.

Marcus Ward & Co., Royal Ulster Works, Belfast.

www.ingramcontent.com/pod-product-compliance
Lightning Source LLC
Chambersburg PA
CBHW030128030726
47498CB00007B/2602